Anybody Home?

Jenny was halfway across the living room when she heard the loud knocking.

She jumped. Her heart seemed to skip a beat.

No, she thought. That's the loose shutter banging against the house.

But it couldn't be. There was no wind.

She heard it again. Four hard raps. Someone was knocking on the front door.

She ran to the door. "Who's there?" she called.

Silence.

An idea flashed into her head. The living room window. Maybe she could see the front porch from the living room window. Maybe she could see who it was from there.

Three more knocks.

She pulled back the heavy drapes. Light from the porch light cast a yellow glow over the front yard.

Suddenly someone leaped up on the other side of the glass, as if being shot up from under the ground.

A scream ripped from Jenny's throat as she saw the hideous, deformed figure staring back at her, his twisted face pressed menacingly against the windowpane.

**Other Point paperbacks
you will enjoy:**

The BABY-SITTER

R.L. Stine

SCHOLASTIC INC.
New York Toronto London Auckland Sydney

ISBN 0-590-44236-8

20 19 18 17   6 7 8 9/9 0/0

Printed in the U.S.A.   01

First Scholastic printing, July 1989

Chapter 1

Jenny stared at her reflection in the dark window glass as the bus squealed around a corner and headed up North Road. Dark houses and trees rushed past in the night. She examined her face in the window, her round, black eyes catching a sparkle from a streetlight and reflecting it back. She liked the way she looked in the glass, so smooth, so cool, so calm.

The bus slowed for a stop sign. What was that animal darting through the hedges? Was it a deer? No. Just a rock. Don't start seeing things, Jenny, she told herself, laughing at her vivid imagination. She was always trying to make the world more interesting than it was.

"Hey — I don't think you've heard a word I'm saying!" Laura's voice broke into her thoughts.

Jenny turned quickly from the window and smiled guiltily at her friend beside her on the bus seat. Laura had been talking nonstop, mostly about boys, as usual, and Jenny, lost in her own thoughts, had practically forgotten she was there. "Sorry. Guess I'm just nervous. It was nice of you to ride partway with me."

"I know," Laura said. "So what are you nervous about? It isn't like you haven't baby-sat before."

"I don't know. I guess it's just new people, a strange house, a strange neighborhood. There's a lot I could worry about if I really put my mind to it." That was supposed to be a joke, but Laura didn't laugh. They'd been friends so long, they didn't have to laugh at each other's jokes.

Jenny glanced at her watch. It was already seven-ten. She didn't want to be late on her first night. The bus hit a deep pothole, and both girls nearly bounced off the plastic bus seat. Jenny leaned forward to retrieve her book bag, which had tumbled onto the floor.

"Maybe the kid's a monster," Jenny said, somehow feeling that she had to justify her nervousness. "Maybe the parents are weird. Maybe they belong to some sort of secret cult and when I find out about it, they keep me locked up in the basement for the rest of my life so I can't tell anyone. Maybe the house is haunted. There's the ghost of a young girl trapped in the attic, and I accidentally let her out, and she inhabits my body and I'm not the same person anymore."

"Possible. Very possible," Laura said thoughtfully. She was used to Jenny's wild imagination. She didn't even bother being sarcastic about it anymore. What was the point? There was no way to stop Jenny from dreaming up the crazy things she did.

"Hey — isn't that Bob Tanner?" Laura cried, pointing out the window.

"Where?"

"That guy, raking the leaves in the dark!" Laura reached past Jenny and struggled to pull up the bus window. It was stuck, and she only managed to raise it an inch. "Hey, Bob! Bob! Hi!" she shouted through the narrow opening.

Jenny looked to the front of the bus to see if the other three passengers were staring at them. They were.

"Hey, Bob! Look up! Hi! Bob!" Why did Laura always have to embarrass her?

Because she was Laura. She didn't care about what other people thought. She always did what she felt like. Jenny wished she could be more like that, less thoughtful, less timid, more impulsive. She thought that since they spent so much time together, maybe some of Laura's boldness would rub off on her. But it didn't seem to.

Sometimes Jenny wished she could look like Laura, too. Laura was so tiny, so light, so perfect. She was the shortest girl in the sophomore class, but that was certainly no handicap because she was also the most beautiful. She had cheekbones like a model, and curly, straw-colored hair that fell down to her shoulders like a waterfall. She had sky-blue eyes and creamy white skin, and a tiny, red, heart-shaped mouth.

Needless to say, Laura was very popular. She could go out with a different guy every night of the week if she wanted — and she usually wanted!

Jenny felt terribly plain next to Laura. She was of average height, which made her nearly a head taller than Laura, but her figure was still extremely boyish. She had dark brown hair which she wore in stylish, long bangs that fell over her left eye, the hairstyle copied from a model she had seen in *Mademoiselle*, large, serious eyes, a long, straight nose (that her mother said was her best feature!), and lips that always seemed to be pouting.

"You shouldn't put yourself down. You look just like that actress Demi Moore," Laura had told her one day.

"Don't be ridiculous," Jenny had said, and then rushed home to look in the mirror and see if Laura was right. "Laura's totally nuts!" she told herself. But she was secretly pleased.

"Hi, Bob! Over here!"

The boy looked up as the bus started to move again. It wasn't Bob Tanner. He didn't look anything like Bob Tanner.

Laura slumped down low in the seat and laughed. "That's okay. I don't even like Bob Tanner. He's a creep."

"What? Why's he a creep?" Jenny asked, glancing at her watch. Seven-fifteen.

"He thinks he's cool just because he's so tall." Laura was always accusing people of thinking they were cool just because they were tall. "Hey — are you going to go out with Chuck?"

The question caught Jenny off guard. She'd been thinking about Chuck a lot, but she hadn't been able to decide anything. "Oh, I don't know. He's such a goof."

"He's funny," Laura said.

"He's a total nut case," Jenny agreed.

"Did you see him in the lunchroom today when he put the hardboiled egg slices over his eyes? He was a riot."

"If I went out with him, he'd probably embarrass me to death," Jenny said, feeling embarrassed just thinking about Chuck and how he was always goofing on things.

"Did you see him dissecting that rubber chicken in biology?" Laura went on, ignoring Jenny's negative attitude. "I thought Mr. Holstrom was going to have a fit!"

"The worst was the day we had the substitute teacher in McNally's class," Jenny said, shaking her head. "Chuck convinced the poor woman that he was deaf, and then he kept talking to her in this dreadful, phony sign language. We were all on the floor. She didn't know what was going on! I felt so sorry for her."

Chuck had only been at Harrison High for a few weeks, but already he was a legendary class clown. When he had come up to Jenny at her locker after school and asked if she'd like to go out sometime, she was startled. She hadn't ever really talked to him except to say hi in the halls or at the beginning of history class. She had put him off, saying she was very busy studying.

Why had she been so reluctant? Because she was reluctant about everything? Because she liked to think about things first, to imagine what they would be like before she actually did them?

Because she preferred imagining things to actually doing them?

No. She was just a cautious person, that's all.

Besides, why should she go out with such a goof? He'd probably spend the whole night showing off and trying to be funny. How boring.

"I don't know. If he asks me again, I might go out with him," she told Laura.

She glanced at her watch again, shook her head impatiently, and stared out the window at a lawn blanketed with shifting, tumbling brown leaves. The tall oaks and maples that bordered the yard were nearly bare. Winter was only a few weeks away.

"So you're going to baby-sit for these people twice a week?" Laura asked.

"Yep. Thursdays and Saturdays."

"How'd you get this job, anyway?"

"It was an accident, really," Jenny replied. "I was at the mall last Saturday with my cousin Melanie. We were just hanging out, not shopping or anything. Then I saw this little boy. He was hard to miss. He had the most amazing blond hair. It was almost pure white, and very straight and shiny. He looked like the kind of kid you see only in TV commercials.

"He was by himself, playing near the fountain, and his toy tank fell into the water. He started to climb in after it.

"I shouted for him to stop. He didn't seem to be with anyone. And he wasn't paying any at-

tention to my shouts. He got up on the ledge over
the fountain and was about to jump in after his
tank. I ran as fast as I could. That fountain's
pretty deep. I grabbed him by the shoulders,
picked him up, and pulled him away.

"He was pretty upset with me for stopping
him. But he got over it as soon as I pulled his
tank out of the water for him. He was the cutest
kid I've ever seen, big blue eyes, so big they
didn't look real, round cheeks, and that amazing
blond hair.

"He thanked me and told me his name was
Donny. I asked him where his mom and dad
were, and he just shrugged. He didn't seem to
care. He told me he was six, but he seemed very
sophisticated for six."

"Kids are sophisticated these days," Laura
said. "My nephew Eddie is only four, and he's
already into girls."

"Well, he seemed just like a little adult to me,"
Jenny continued. "He was so cute. Melanie had
to leave, but I wanted to stay with him until his
parents found him. He and I sat down by the
fountain and had a nice talk, mostly about toys.
I think he wanted to tell me every toy he had at
home and every toy he wanted for Christmas."

"So then Donny's parents came?"

"Yeah. A few minutes later. And did they look
relieved to see him! It turned out they'd been
searching for him for nearly twenty minutes.
They were frantic, and he didn't even look up
when they came. He just wanted to keep talking
with me.

"Mr. Hagen introduced himself and his wife. Then he said, 'Well, you and Donny really seem to have hit it off.' Then Donny asked if he could bring me home with him!

"We all laughed. Then Mr. Hagen said that actually they *were* looking for a baby-sitter, someone to come and stay with Donny every Thursday and Saturday night. He asked if I might be interested in the job.

"Well, of course I started to say no."

"Why?" Laura asked.

"I don't know. Because I always say no when I'm asked something the first time, I guess. I like time to think things over. But Donny started begging me to say yes. He was so cute. And I knew Mom and I could really use the money. The Hagens seemed like okay people. So I said yes, I'd give it a try.

"Then Donny started leaping up and down for joy and almost fell into the fountain again!"

"Oh, no!" Laura suddenly jumped up. "My stop!" She lurched toward the front of the bus. "Hey, stop! Please! My stop!"

The bus driver slammed on the brakes. Laura saved herself from flying the rest of the way by grabbing a pole. She turned back to Jenny. " 'Bye! Call me later. Good luck!" And she hopped down the steps and out the door.

The bus pulled away. Jenny looked nervously at her watch. Seven twenty-five. No way she'd be there on time at seven-thirty. She stared into the dark glass and watched the houses glide by. It was a long ride from her house across town to the Old Village where the Hagens lived. She'd have to remember to leave earlier on Saturday night. If she was going to make this trip twice a week, she had to get the timing right.

A few minutes later, the bus pulled into Millertown Road and Jenny, still staring at her dark reflection in the window glass, nearly missed her stop. Suddenly realizing where she was, she pulled the bell cord and ran up to the front door just as the driver was about to pull away.

Bad start, she told herself, stepping down into the cool night air. She squinted up at the street signs, which were partially covered by low-hanging tree branches. Then, following the Hagens' directions, she turned right and headed down Edgetown Lane.

Three blocks to go, she told herself. She started jogging. She was about ten minutes late. The houses she passed were old and very large, mostly Colonial style, with wide, landscaped lawns and majestic old trees that bowed in the wind, as if watching her pass by.

The blocks were long. The houses gave way to woods. A small black dog came running up from behind her, yapping and sniffing at her sneakers as she ran. "Go home, dog. Go home," she said, already out of breath, a sense of dread growing from the pit of her stomach, slowing her steps, making her legs feel as if they weighed a thousand pounds. Yipping excitedly, the dog gave a last snap, just missing her ankle, and turned back into the woods.

She crossed the empty street. The Hagens'

house should be in the next block. She slowed to a walk and tried to catch her breath. On the corner stood a low ranch-style house, completely dark, the hedge ragged and overgrown, the leaves still unraked. That wasn't it.

The wind picked up. Jenny pulled up the collar of her jean jacket and adjusted her backpack. She passed by a narrow lot of tangled trees and low brambles. Just past the lot, a mailbox on a pole jutted out into the street. Jenny was relieved to see the name HAGEN painted on its side.

She looked up the long driveway to the house. A porch light was on, casting pale white light against the dark, mottled shingles. The house was enormous, a rambling old Victorian. Even at first glance, it seemed rundown. A loose shutter banged loudly against an upstairs window. Another shutter had fallen at an angle and was hanging by only one hinge. A window at the far end of the house had been broken, the hole filled in with balled-up newspapers.

Oh, great. The house is right out of a horror movie, Jenny thought. There's probably green slime pouring out of the walls!

She looked at her watch. Fifteen minutes late. She didn't have time to be worrying about broken windows or green slime. She ran up the drive, the crunch of her sneakers on the gravel the only sound except for the wind.

She stepped into the white light of the porch, straightened her hair, pulling the long bangs down over her left eye, adjusted her backpack, cleared her throat, prepared a smile to greet the Hagens with, and rang the doorbell.

The bell didn't work. So she knocked, having to bang with all her strength to make a sound against the hard, thick wood. She heard footsteps inside.

Okay, kiddo, she told herself. Break a leg.

Chapter 2

"Come in, Jenny. Come in. We were just starting to worry about you." Mr. Hagen pushed open the storm door and stepped aside so that Jenny could enter the narrow front hallway. "Getting chilly out there. Is that jacket warm enough? Did you have trouble finding the place?"

"No. Sorry I'm late. The bus — "

"Let me take your jacket," he interrupted, pulling at the sleeve before she could remove her backpack. "The coat closet door is jammed shut, so I'll put it in our bedroom closet upstairs. Okay? As you can see, the house needs a bit of work. We just moved in a few months ago. The house was built before the Civil War — can you believe it? Well, I can. It looks as if no one did any work on it since then! Ha ha!"

Jenny laughed politely and struggled to get the jean jacket off.

Didn't he ever take a breath? He seemed terribly nervous, not at all like at the mall the weekend before.

Mr. Hagen was a big man, so tall he had to stoop in the low entranceway. He was built wide with big shoulders and powerful-looking hands. He was good-looking in a square-jawed, old-fashioned kind of way. He was wearing a charcoal-gray suit which was snug against his broad chest. His dark hair was cut short, almost a crew cut, and thinning just a bit in front. His eyes were small and steel-gray, and never seemed to stop darting about. His cheeks and ears were red, whether from excitement, or nervousness, or just their natural hue, Jenny couldn't tell.

As he hurried off to take her jacket upstairs, Jenny noticed that he walked with a slight limp. She didn't remember that from the mall, either. But of course she had only seen the Hagens for a few minutes there by the fountain.

"Oh, hi, Jenny. Where is Mike off to?" Mrs. Hagen walked quickly into the hallway, her rimless glasses catching the overhead light and reflecting it so that her small face seemed to radiate light. She was tall and thin, sort of homey, down-to-earth-looking, Jenny thought, with short, curly brown hair and those rimless glasses that hid her large, brown eyes. She wore a simple white peasant blouse and a dark wraparound skirt, clothes that made her look older than she was.

"He took my jacket upstairs. Sorry, I'm late. The bus — "

"Oh, that's okay. We have plenty of time. Don't pay any attention to Mike. He's always nervous on the nights we go out. No. Change that. He's always nervous. Period. But you'll get used to him."

"I heard that!" Mr. Hagen called from the top of the stairway.

"Where's Donny?" Jenny asked, picking her backpack up off the floor.

"He's in the den watching a tape. *Ghostbusters*, I think. He's seen it six hundred times. He says it's awesome." She laughed. "It's funny how all of the trendy words and phrases, you know, words like awesome, drift down to the six-year-olds about two years after they've gone out of style. I keep waiting for Donny to tell me that some movie is real groovy, but that word hasn't caught up with him yet. Or maybe it passed him by. I was a linguistics major, believe it or not. So I'm very interested in words and how they travel."

"Really," Jenny said. Then she felt like a jerk. Really? Was that the best she could do? Really??

"Hey, Donny — look who's here," Mrs. Hagen called.

Jenny followed her through the large, cluttered living room. The living room furniture seemed as ramshackle and rundown as the rest of the house. The sofa cushions didn't exactly match, and a large, peach-colored, overstuffed armchair had one arm that appeared to be held in place with masking tape.

"Don't mind the furniture," Mrs. Hagen said, catching the surprised look on Jenny's face. "We inherited it with the house. We're redoing the whole room as soon as Mike gets established at his new job." She continued to the den and motioned for Jenny to follow her in. "Donny, look who's here to stay with you."

Donny was lying on his stomach on the carpet in front of the TV. He didn't look up. "Quiet," he said. "This is a good part. Venkman is gonna get it."

"Donny, don't be rude," Mrs. Hagen said. "You can at least look up from the TV for one second and say hi to Jenny."

"Hi," Donny said without looking away from the screen.

"I guess the romance is over. How quickly they forget," Jenny said with mock sadness.

Mrs. Hagen laughed. "He's impossible," she said.

"No, I'm not," Donny muttered, engrossed in Venkman's battle against the slimy green ghost.

"We're going to be late," Mr. Hagen said impatiently, bursting into the den and shoving his wife's coat at her. "Donny, you have to go to bed when the movie's over."

"Aw, Dad. I didn't have any time to play. Can't I stay up just a little?"

"Well . . . maybe a little. But you have to listen to what Jenny tells you." Mr. Hagen turned to Jenny. His ears and cheeks were bright scarlet. "I'm sorry I didn't have a chance to show you around. I'm sure you won't have any trouble. Donny can give you the grand tour after his movie."

"I'll be fine," Jenny said, looking at Donny.

"We won't be too late," Mr. Hagen continued, talking rapidly. "I left the number where we can be reached in the kitchen. Call if you have any problem at all. Donny can show you how to operate the VCR if you want to watch a tape or something. We're not expecting any phone calls, but in case — "

"Really, Mike," Mrs. Hagen scolded, "I'm sure Jenny has baby-sat before — haven't you, dear?"

"Yes, of course," Jenny said, giving them her most confident smile.

"Here comes a good part," Donny shouted over several loud, explosive blasts from the movie soundtrack. "Awesome! Awesome!"

"Well, if you have any problems at all, the number is on the pad by the phone in the kitchen," Mr. Hagen continued undaunted. "Donny will show you where the kitchen is. And by all means, be sure to keep all the doors locked. Did you read in the paper about the attacks on baby-sitters in this town?" He shook his head sadly and sighed. "Some world we live in."

"I saw it on the news," Jenny said softly. Some creep in a ski mask was breaking into homes and beating up baby-sitters. So far, there had been two attacks. Both baby-sitters had had to be hospitalized.

After she saw the news stories, Jenny decided not to take the job with the Hagens. Her imagination ran wild and she pictured hideous, horrifying scenes. But then she forced herself to think about it clearly. What were the chances the attacker would choose the Hagen house way over on the far end of town? One in ten thousand? No — one in a million!

If I keep the doors locked, I'll be perfectly safe, she told herself. And, besides, she really needed the money. . . .

"Mike, why on earth did you have to bring that up? Are you trying to make Jenny nervous on her first night? Come on. You've said more than enough. Move on out." Mrs. Hagen gave Jenny a conspiratorial wink and shoved her husband hard from behind. He didn't budge. It was like trying to move a tank.

"Good night, Donny. Be good," both parents called as they headed to the front door.

Donny didn't reply.

Jenny slipped into a soft, white leather armchair against the wall. "You're sitting awfully close," she told Donny. His face was only a few inches from the screen.

"I'm allowed," he said. He watched the movie for a while. Jenny watched him. She just couldn't get over his beautiful blond hair. It was so smooth and wonderfully-shaped like a perfect golden bowl, so shiny, so fine.

"Do you like *Ghostbusters*?" he asked.

"I haven't seen it for a few years," she told him.

The front door slammed. The Hagens had left.

Donny turned away from the TV screen and actually looked at Jenny for the first time. "Did

17

they leave?" he asked, looking concerned.

"Yes," she told him. "They just left."

"Good," he said. "Can I have a candy bar?"

Getting Donny to bed wasn't as hard as Jenny had predicted. He was a very lively, active kid, and when he finally got tired he just suddenly crashed, his energy all used up, barely enough strength left to keep his eyelids up.

Jenny took him up to his room and tucked him in. "See you on Saturday night," she whispered, running her hand tenderly through his amazing hair.

He was nearly asleep before she turned out the light and crept out of the room.

The carpet on the stairs was worn right through to the wood in several places. The stairs creaked beneath her feet as she descended to the living room.

What a creepy old place. Why did people think it was neat to live in 200-year-old houses? When I have my own home, Jenny decided, it's going to be sparkling and brand new.

She stopped in the living room to look around. Everything smelled so musty. The floor creaked as she walked. A tall, mahogany grandfather's clock in the corner ticked, then tocked, loudly, insistently.

I'd go nuts if I had to listen to that all day, Jenny thought.

She suddenly imagined the original owners of the house, sitting by the fire, listening to the ticktocking of the big clock. The ghostly pale woman was dressed in black except for a white bonnet on her head and a gray wool shawl over her shoulders. She sat knitting another gray wool shawl. The man was also dressed in black. He had a long, white beard and mustache. He stood by the fireplace, staring at an enormous, dripping red hog being roasted on a spit in the fireplace. "Just think," he said softly, "more than a hundred years from now, that clock of ours is going to drive whoever's in this house bananas!"

BAAAAM!

A loud banging noise made Jenny jump. Her fantasy old-time couple vanished. What was *that*?

Then she remembered the loose shutter on the front of the house. She walked to the window, pushed back the heavy, crushed-velvet drapes, and looked out.

The darkness seemed thick enough to touch. Swaying trees were black shadows against the black sky. The house appeared to be surrounded by woods. She couldn't see another house, another car, another sign of human life. Her eyes adjusted to the darkness outside, but there was only more darkness to see.

She shivered. It was drafty by the window. One of the panes was cracked, and cold air was seeping in all around the window frame.

Somewhere not too far away an animal howled. Was it a dog? Please, she thought, let it be a dog. The shutter banged again, harder this time. Again, she jumped.

She stepped back and rearranged the heavy drapes. Tick Tock. Tick TOCK. The annoying clock seemed to grow louder. She heard a soft cracking sound above her head. The house groaned and shifted as the winds picked up outside.

Take it easy, she told herself. All old houses make weird sounds. She was sorry she had put Donny to bed. The noises weren't so loud or frightening when he was around. When she was playing with him, she didn't have time to think about where she was, all alone in this creepy, old house surrounded by nothing but dark woods.

She looked up at the wall above the mantel. A hideous moose head, its fur caked with dust and mold, seemed to glare down at her. The grandfather's clock chimed loudly, nine o'clock, tick TOCK, tick TOCK, its pendulum swinging quickly back and forth, clicking the time away.

Jenny decided to check out the kitchen. She turned toward the hall — and something grabbed her leg.

Chapter 3

She screamed.

The ghost of the lady in the gray shawl had her by the leg.

Now she was going to carry Jenny into the clock, where she would live forever, listening for all of eternity to the tick TOCK tick TOCK along with the other spirits of this old house.

She looked down.

It wasn't a ghost. It was a ginger-colored cat. The cat pawed her again, softer this time, then rubbed its back against her jeans leg, mewing loudly.

Jenny's heart was still pounding.

Why didn't they tell me they had a cat?

She reached down to pet it, but it ran away, tucking itself under a large sofa.

She felt foolish screaming like that. She wasn't the screaming type. She took a deep breath and held it, a trick that usually worked when she wanted to calm herself.

Had her scream disturbed Donny?

She ran up the creaking stairs and tiptoed into his room. He was still sleeping peacefully. He looked even more angelic when he slept. She was tempted to wake him up, tell him he could come downstairs and play until his parents came home.

No, Jenny. You've got to show them you're responsible.

She heard the animal howls again, closer this time, louder and longer. They seemed to be coming from the backyard. She crept over to Donny's window, pushed back the curtains, and looked down.

A spotlight on the side of the garage cast a narrow triangle of yellow light over the gravel driveway, a low woodpile, and the tall grass of the yard. Shadows from the trees danced over the grass, which leaned first this way, then that in the swirling wind.

The howling had stopped.

Jenny replaced the curtains, took one more look at Donny, then walked quickly downstairs. She found the kitchen, the last room off the long, back hallway, and turned on all the lights. It was the only modern room in the house, bright yellow and orange linoleum tile on the floor, newly painted white wooden cabinets, new appliances, even a microwave.

I guess this is the only room they've been able to redo, Jenny told herself. She found a Coke in the refrigerator and a bag of nacho chips on the counter. Maybe I'll just stay in the kitchen all night, she thought. It's so much less creepy in here.

But the kitchen stools were uncomfortable, and she had left her backpack in the den. And she realized that from way in the back of the house she wouldn't be able to hear Donny if he called from upstairs. So she carried her snack back down the long hallway, through the living room with its creaking floors and annoying clock, and back to the den.

Well, what shall I do now? she asked herself, dropping back down into the big white leather chair. I can't just sit around and listen to the wind howl and the shutters bang, and think about how creepy it is here.

She picked up the newspaper from the table next to the chair and scanned the front page. "Oh!" A headline made her gasp. *THIRD BABY-SITTER ATTACK HAS POLICE ON ALERT.* She tossed the paper down without reading the story.

Then she remembered that before leaving the house she had grabbed a book to read. But what was it? She searched in her pack and pulled it out. Oh, great. A Stephen King novel. Good choice, Jenny. That'll really cheer you up!

She stuffed the book back into her pack and got up. Should she switch on the TV? No. She couldn't sit still. She decided to explore the living room for a while.

She was walking past the soot-stained, marble fireplace in front of the sofa with the cushions that didn't match when she heard the first footstep.

She stopped.

She wasn't sure she had heard it.

Yes. Another. This time she was sure. It was a footstep. A soft footstep.

The cat again?

No. The cat was curled up in a chair by the window.

She listened. Silence now. So silent except for her breathing, except for the pounding of her heart, except for the ticking of the clock.

So, she had imagined it.

Another ghost, another creature of her imagination.

"Stop it, Jenny," she said aloud. "Stop imagining things. It's scary enough here without you trying to scare yourself."

Another footstep.

This one louder.

This one closer.

Someone was in the house. Someone was walking quietly . . . slowly . . . deliberately.

She spun around and looked back to the den. Could she get there in time? Could she lock herself in the den? Could she call the police? Would they get to the house in time?

Another footstep.

She turned back to face the front hallway.

The footsteps were coming from the stairs.

She froze. She felt completely paralyzed, paralyzed by fear. So this is what it's like, she thought. So this is what it's like to be frightened to death.

An image flashed into her mind. She was driving home with her mom late at night. They were in the old Pontiac. She must have been five or six. They pulled into the driveway. A rabbit was standing at the top of the drive. Caught in the headlights, it froze. The poor creature became paralyzed, a statue of fear. It stood there staring into the headlights as the car came closer and closer. It didn't move a muscle until Jenny's mom turned the headlights off. Then it bounded away, its long ears standing straight up in the air.

Another footstep on the stairs.

Jenny was the rabbit now, frozen in front of the fireplace.

She wanted to move. She wanted to run. She wanted to scream.

But her fear held her in a tight grip.

"Who — " She finally managed to make a sound. "Who's there?"

Silence.

Another footstep.

"Who's there?" she called.

Chapter 4

"Who's there?"

Donny stepped into the hallway. His cheeks were flushed from sleep. He had red leather slippers on his feet. One pajama leg had hitched up over his knee. "I woke up. I'm thirsty."

Jenny took a deep breath. Her knees felt weak. She grabbed onto the mantel to steady herself. She didn't want Donny to see that she had been afraid.

She felt like laughing. Then she felt like crying. Then she felt like running up and hugging him.

What an idiot she had been! Footsteps. Of *course* there were footsteps on the stairs. How could Donny come down the stairs without making footsteps? How could she have forgotten that she wasn't alone in the house?

He stared at her from the entranceway to the living room. "I'm thirsty," he repeated. His voice was hoarse from sleep. He had a very devilish look on his face.

She walked over to him and smoothed her hand through his hair. "You shouldn't sneak down the stairs."

"I didn't sneak. I walked. Slowly. I didn't know where you were. I didn't want to scare you."

Didn't want to scare her?!

She squeezed his shoulder playfully. He giggled. "Are you *sure* you didn't want to scare me?" she asked.

"Well . . . maybe a little." He giggled some more.

"Are you the kind of guy who likes scaring his baby-sitters?" she asked, starting to feel a little more normal.

"Maybe."

They headed toward the kitchen, her hand on his pajama shoulder. He felt so warm, like a little stove.

"Well, I'm glad to see you," she said. What an understatement! "What do you want to drink? Apple juice?"

"No. I brushed my teeth tonight."

"So?"

"So, apple juice tastes funny after you brush your teeth. I want milk."

"Okay. Milk, it is."

In the kitchen, he climbed up on one of the stools while she poured out his glass of milk. He drank it quickly in three long gulps, then wiped the milk mustache off his upper lip with the sleeve of his pajamas.

"Want to play a game or something?" he asked.

"Get serious. You get right back up to bed," she told him. "Did your other baby-sitters play games with you late at night?"

"Maybe," he said, the devilish grin reappearing.

"Tell the truth, Donny," Jenny said with mock sternness.

"Well . . . no," he admitted sheepishly. Then he quickly added, "I'll only go back to bed if you'll tuck me in again."

"Okay. That's a deal," Jenny agreed.

It took a long time to tuck him in. First he insisted on showing her all of his stuffed animals and telling her their names. When she finally got him into bed and under the covers, he said, "Kiss me good night."

She bent down and kissed him on the forehead. "Good night."

"Now tell me a story," he demanded.

"What?"

"Tell me a story. I can't go to sleep without a story."

"But, Donny, that wasn't the deal. The deal was for me to tuck you in."

"Now the deal is for you to tell me a story," he insisted. She saw that he was a tough bargainer. There was probably no use in arguing with him.

"What kind of stories do you like?" she asked,

sighing resignedly and settling down at the foot of his narrow, stuffed animal-cluttered bed.

"Scary stories."

Of course.

"Okay. Let me think." She didn't have to think too long. She was good at thinking up stories. It was one of the real advantages of having a wild imagination.

"This is a story about a little boy who liked to scare his baby-sitter," she began.

Donny laughed. "I like it," he said, sitting up.

"If you don't lie down and try to sleep, I won't finish it," Jenny threatened. He plopped back onto his pillow. "This little boy was about your age, about your height, just about your weight. In fact, he looked just like you." She scooted up closer to him so she could whisper the story.

"And this little boy had a very mischievous personality. He liked playing tricks on his baby-sitter and scaring her to death. He would sneak down the stairs as quietly as he could just to frighten her. He would make loud noises and jump out at her from dark doorways and run into the room and leap onto her shoulders from behind when she thought he was sound asleep.

"One night, he scared his baby-sitter so badly, her hair turned white. And one night, he scared his baby-sitter so badly, her eyes popped out, and he had to find them and push them back in for her. And one night, he scared his baby-sitter so badly, she jumped right out of her skin — and it took her hours to put it back on."

Donny thought this was hilarious. He laughed

29

until he had tears in his eyes. He made Jenny tell that part again. And then again.

"So one night the little boy's baby-sitter decided to get even. She decided that it was her turn to scare the little boy."

Jenny scooted even closer so she could whisper as quietly as possible. "She thought and thought about how to scare the little boy. Should she dress up in a gorilla costume and pop out of his clothes closet? No. Not scary enough. Should she invite a monster to come in and chase the little boy around the house? No. Not scary enough. Should she take off her skin again and dance around in her bones? No. Not scary enough."

Jenny leaned down very close to Donny's ear and softly whispered the conclusion to her story. "And then the baby-sitter finally got an idea. She finally thought of the scariest trick of all. Very quietly, she crept into the little boy's bedroom. Very quietly, she leaned down over his bed where he was about to fall asleep. And very quietly, quiet as a mouse, almost silently, almost as silent as a soft breeze, almost so silently you couldn't hear her, she shouted, 'BOOOOOOOOOOO!'"

Jenny shouted the word *boo* at the top of her lungs.

The story received the proper reaction. Donny leaped up in surprise and nearly fell out of bed. Then he laughed uproariously. "Tell it again," he insisted when he had finally stopped laughing.

Pleased with her success, Jenny headed to the bedroom door. "No. Go to sleep now."

"Come on, Jenny. Tell it again."

"No. Next time. I'll be back on Saturday night. I'll tell it to you then. Only I'll make it scarier."

He made her promise three times that she wouldn't forget. Then he finally settled down to go to sleep.

Jenny was smiling as she started down the stairs. "That was a good story," she told herself. "I'm going to be good at this job." The thought gave her special pleasure. Her mother was always accusing her of being irresponsible, of living in a world of daydreams and not being able to handle anything real. But her mother was wrong. Jenny was proving that.

Her smile faded when she heard the loud knock on the front door. She stopped on the bottom step and grabbed the bannister. She could feel the fear grip her body, the same fear she had felt in the living room when she had heard the quiet footsteps.

The knock was repeated, harder this time.

Who could it be?

It was too early for the Hagens to be home. And they wouldn't knock.

Could she see out? No. The door was solid wood, no window or peephole.

Whoever was out there pounded again, three hard raps, then three more.

It sounds like a burglar, Jenny thought. A picture of a guy in a black-and-purple striped sweater, wearing a black mask over his eyes, carrying a bag of burglar tools flashed into her mind.

No. It's not a burglar. A burglar wouldn't knock.

Unless it was a very cautious burglar, and he was checking to make sure no one was home before breaking in. So if I don't answer the door, he'll think no one is home, and he'll —

It's the baby-sitter attacker, the one in the papers.

No. Don't be stupid. How would he know there's a baby-sitter here tonight? It's my first night on the job.

It's the police. A truck carrying toxic waste turned over outside, and they have to evacuate the neighborhood immediately. If I don't answer the door, I'll breathe the toxic fumes and be turned into a drooling mutant. . . .

Three more hard raps on the door.

Jenny pressed her cheek against the door. The wood felt surprisingly cold. "Who is it?"

No reply.

She could hear the wind roaring outside the door.

"Who is it?" she repeated. She didn't want to shout too loudly for fear of waking up Donny.

"Who is it? Who's there?"

She pressed her ear against the door again. The wind was howling too loudly to hear anything else.

"I'd better open the door," she told herself. She looked for a chain to attach so that an intruder couldn't just push his way in. But there was none.

Three more knocks.

She took a deep breath and pulled the door open a crack.

"Oh." The cry escaped her lips before she could stop it.

The white porch light revealed a short but powerfully built man. Despite the cold and gusting winds, he was wearing only an oversized, red plaid lumberjack shirt. His eyebrows caught Jenny's attention first. They were bushy and black, as wide as caterpillars. He had thick black hair slicked down with some kind of grease and brushed straight back so that it looked more like a helmet than hair.

His nose was bent and leaned to the left. It looked as if it had been broken several times, or maybe removed and put back on wrong. He had a stubble of black beard on his cheeks, and an unlit stub of a cigar tucked between his teeth. He reeked of the aroma of cigars. It must have been soaked into his shirt and jeans.

He looked as startled to see Jenny as she was to see him. "Who are *you*?" he asked, his voice surprisingly deep but gravelly. Somehow he was able to speak and still keep the cigar butt clamped between his teeth.

"I — I'm the baby-sitter," Jenny said, struggling to remember exactly who she was. "Who are you?"

He looked at her suspiciously. He didn't seem to hear her question. "Everything okay in there?"

"Yes," she said, squeezing the doorknob until her hand hurt. "Can I help you with something?"

Dumb question, but what else should she say?

"No. Uh . . . I'm sorry. I'm Willers. I'm the neighbor."

"Oh. The neighbor." Jenny started to feel a little relieved. But then she thought, maybe he's lying, and her fear returned.

"I thought Mike and Mary were home." He chewed on the cigar butt and looked her up and down.

"Uh . . . no. They're out tonight. They go out on Thursday nights."

Why did I tell him that? How stupid! Now he knows that I'll be alone here with Donny every Thursday night. Stupid, stupid, stupid.

"I'm sorry to disturb you this time of night. I thought I saw a prowler out back." He pointed a stubby finger toward the woods on the right. "Did you happen to hear anything?"

"No. Not a thing."

Was he really the neighbor? Did he really hear a prowler? Was *he* the prowler?

"I thought I saw someone. There's been a prowler in the neighborhood." He removed the tiny cigar butt from his teeth and jammed it into his shirt pocket. "Mind if I come in and look around?"

"Yes. I mean no. I don't think so. I mean, I don't know you. I don't think the Hagens would. . . . I mean, everything's okay. I didn't hear anything."

He squinted at her suspiciously, his thick, black eyebrows folding above his eyes like upside-down V's. "You sure?"

"Yes. Positive. It was nice of you to be concerned, though. Thank you."

She started to close the door. He took a step forward.

Her heart jumped up to her throat.

Was he going to try to push his way in? What was he going to do?

Why was he staring at her like that?

"If you hear anything, I'll be nearby," he said, backing down. He looked into her eyes. "I'm always nearby."

Was that a threat?

Why did he stare at her like that when he said it?

Or was she just imagining that he meant more than he said?

"Good night," she said. She closed the door quickly, slamming it hard without realizing it, and locked it. Then she slumped down on the first step and buried her head in her arms, trying to catch her breath.

"YAAAAAIIII!"

She screamed when she felt the hand on her shoulder.

"Sorry. I didn't mean to scare you," Donny said. "I'm thirsty again."

Chapter 5

"So did you mmpfell the mmmpphh about the nmmmmphh?"

"What? I can't understand you, Laura."

Laura held up a finger, signalling for Jenny to wait a second while she finished swallowing. "I had a mouthful of pizza. Sorry. What I said was, did you tell the father about the neighbor?"

"Tell Mr. Hagen? No. He's much too nervous already. I didn't want to make him more nervous. Besides, what's to tell? The neighbor came over to make sure everything was okay. Big deal."

"But, Jenny, you said you thought — "

"But that's my problem, don't you see? I'm always thinking too much, thinking crazy things. So the neighbor was a little shifty-looking. Lots of neighbors are shifty-looking. It doesn't mean they're going to break into the house and cut you up in little pieces or anything."

"Mmmmphhh wwwmmmmphh," Laura replied.

"Huh?"

They were sitting in the back booth at the Pizza Oven. It was three-thirty on Friday afternoon, and the small restaurant was usually filled with Harrison High students by now. But for some reason only a few kids were there today. Jenny and Laura liked the back booth despite the torn seat cushions and the fact that it was directly across from the restroom, because from there they could see who was in all the other booths and who came in the door, without being easily seen themselves.

"Do you think this is real cheese?" Laura pulled a long strand of it with two fingers. It stretched for about two feet before it tore.

"I don't know. Of course. What else would it be?"

"I saw on TV where some pizza places were using fake cheese. You know, artificial cheese, all chemicals and stuff."

"It tastes like cheese. A little," Jenny said, taking a large bite for scientific purposes. "Why do you always have such upsetting news? I mean, if you can't believe in pizza, what can you believe in?"

"I'd like to believe in *him*," Laura said, dropping her pizza slice to stare at a tall boy with wavy blond hair, wearing tight-fitting 501s and a leather bomber jacket. "Who is he? Look at that smile. He looks like he just walked off a movie set."

"Never seen him," Jenny said, concentrating on her pizza. She'd been starving all day. "What's with you and Eugene?"

"Who?"

"Laura — stop staring at him like that."

"You think I'm being too obvious?"

"Well . . . the staring part isn't so bad," Jenny told her, "but the drooling is not very subtle. I asked you about Eugene."

"I think I'm going to break up with him."

"What?"

"Well, I think I have to. You'll never guess who asked me out."

"Who?"

"Promise you won't laugh."

"What? Okay, Laura. I promise. I mean, I'll try. Who?"

"Bob Tanner."

"You're joking!"

"Stop laughing!"

"But you said he was too tall — "

"Well, he sort of stooped over when he asked me out."

"But I thought you and Eugene were — "

"Finished. It just got stale, know what I mean? We were only going out together because we couldn't think of anything else to do."

They've been going together for two weeks, Jenny thought. And it got stale?

But she didn't say what she was thinking. Laura was so beautiful, she really could have any boy she wanted. But Jenny thought it was kind of sad that Laura wanted them all. At the end of summer, Laura had broken up with Rick Danielson. That had lasted nearly three months, a long time for Laura. Since then, she'd gone out with at least three other guys. Now Eugene was about to be dumped.

I'd settle for just one guy, Jenny thought, one serious guy. Again, she felt plain and boring compared to Laura. Why couldn't she stare at boys the way Laura did, or touch their shoulders all the time the way Laura did, or act real kittenish and sexy and not get embarrassed about it?

She took another bite of pizza. It had no taste at all. Maybe the Pizza Oven did use artificial cheese. Yeccch.

"So, are you keeping this job?" Laura asked. The blond boy in the bomber jacket had walked out with a tall, black-haired girl, so Laura's attention returned to Jenny.

"I guess so. Sure," Jenny said. "They're paying me five dollars an hour since it's so far away from my house. I can really use the money. I'll actually be able to buy people Christmas presents this year. And I can help Mom out a little."

"But you said the place was creepy, and you were scared to death, what with the weird neighbor and everything."

"It was all in my mind, Laura. It was all just me. I got terrified because I heard footsteps, and they turned out to be Donny's footsteps. There wasn't anything to really be afraid of. The neighbor was perfectly fine, too. If I hadn't already been in such a state, he wouldn't have frightened me at all. I frightened myself, that's all. Next time I'll be cool."

"And the kid isn't a monster?"

"No. He's adorable. I think he likes scaring

the baby-sitter, though. It's sort of a game with him. I'm going to have to talk to him about that. But he's fine, just fine. His father is a bit of a basket case, though."

Laura took a long sip of her Coke. "What do you mean?"

"He's just such a worrier. I guess those news stories about the attacks on baby-sitters have gotten him upset, or something. I don't know. He drove me home, and all the way back he kept asking me, 'Did it go okay? Was everything okay? Was Donny okay?' He must've asked me two dozen times."

"Maybe he was just nervous because it was your first night."

"Yeah, maybe. Maybe he'll calm down. He's very devoted to Donny. It's easy to see that. And his wife is really nice. She just makes jokes about how nervous Mr. Hagen is and what a worrier he is. I guess she's used to it."

"Well . . . it's rough, giving up all your Saturday nights," Laura said, looking toward the front as a group of Harrison kids came in, laughing loudly and shoving each other through the door.

"Not really," Jenny said. "Not for me." She didn't mean to sound quite as gloomy as she did. She looked away.

"Did you save me any pepperoni?" a boy's voice said, nearby.

Jenny and Laura both cried out. Where was the voice coming from?

Suddenly Chuck, a wide grin on his freckled

face, pulled himself up from under their table. He looked very pleased that he had startled them both. He stopped about halfway up and rested his chin on the tabletop.

"Chuck! What were you doing down there?" Laura shrieked.

"Nothing. Just looking up your dress. Ha ha!" His grin grew wider. His blue eyes actually seemed to light up, as if the electricity had just been turned on.

"You idiot!" Laura cried. "Hey — I'm not wearing a dress."

"Then I don't know *what* I was doing down there," Chuck said.

"How long were you down there?" Jenny asked, appalled at the thought that he may have been eavesdropping on their conversation, trying to remember if they'd said anything really embarrassing.

"Since Tuesday, I think." He pulled himself up and squeezed in beside Jenny. "No — don't move," he told her. He put his arm around her shoulder. "I'm comfortable like this." He beamed at her, four hundred perfect white teeth in her face.

"Glad one of us is," Jenny said sarcastically. She took his hand with both of hers and lifted it off her shoulder. He had large hands, she noticed. He was a big guy. Big shoulders, powerful-looking arms. He looked like a football lineman, or a wrestler.

He grabbed up the rest of the pizza on her plate, a tiny sliver, mostly crust. "Our first pizza together," he said, holding it up as if it were a prize. "I'm going to rush home and paste this in my memory book." He stuffed it into his jeans pocket. "I have a very messy memory book."

"Your mother must love to wash your jeans," Jenny said.

"I live with my dad. I wash my own jeans," Chuck said, surprising Jenny by saying something serious.

"I've got to get home," Laura said, starting to climb out of the narrow booth.

"Oh, no," Jenny protested. "You're not leaving me here with him, are you?" She meant it as a joke, sort of. She hoped it came across that way. She looked at Chuck. He didn't seem hurt. Maybe he was used to having girls say that about him.

"I thought she'd never leave," he said loudly, ignoring Jenny's plea and ignoring the fact that Laura hadn't left yet. He put his heavy arm back around Jenny's shoulder.

"Really. I've got to get home," Laura repeated, still not standing up.

"It's been real," Chuck said. "Real gross. Ha ha!"

Jenny laughed. Laura gave her a surprised look. "You think that's funny? It's pitiful."

"It's kind of funny," Jenny said.

Chuck pulled the pizza crust from his pocket and ate it.

"Later," Laura said. She stood up, pulled on her maroon-and-white Harrison High sweatshirt, gave Jenny a meaningful look, and headed to the door.

Jenny looked down at the red Formica table. Should she try having a conversation with Chuck, or should she make an excuse and leave, too? Was it possible to really talk to him, or would he just make nonstop jokes the whole time?

How was she going to get his arm off her shoulder? It weighed at least a ton!

"Could you scoot over to the other side?" she asked, deciding to try to talk with him for a short while.

"You want me to stay?" He looked very surprised. He scratched his curly blond hair, and pulled himself around to the other side of the booth so that he was now facing her.

"When did you move to Harrison?" Jenny asked. It was a test question to see if he could be serious.

"My dad and I came here from Mars a little more than a month ago."

Uh oh. He was flunking the test.

"And what kind of spaceship did you fly in?" Jenny asked, rolling her eyes. "Did you come to defeat our planet, or on a peace mission, or what?"

"No, really," he insisted. "We came from Mars. It's just north of Pittsburgh. In Pennsylvania."

"You're putting me on, right?"

He laughed. He had a dimple in his right cheek when he laughed. With the curly blond hair and all the freckles on his face, he looked like Huck Finn. Jenny decided he was kind of cute. But also kind of goofy-looking.

He raised his right hand. "I swear. I come from Mars. You can look it up on any map. It's near Frisco."

"Near San Francisco?"

"No. Near Frisco. Frisco, Pennsylvania." He raised his hand again. "No joke. I'll swear on my mother's grave."

"Your mother's dead?"

"Well . . . no."

They both laughed.

"I still think you're putting me on," Jenny said.

"I'll bring you a map of Pennsylvania. I'll prove it to you. It's a real tiny town. It's on the old Baltimore and Ohio railroad line. There's not much there. The name is the only interesting thing about the place."

"There must be something wrong with me. I'm starting to believe you," Jenny said.

Chuck just smiled back at her.

The waitress interrupted to ask if they wanted anything else. Chuck ordered a pepperoni pizza. "That should be enough for me. Can I get you anything?" he joked.

"Make it two," Jenny joked.

The waitress wrote it down on her pad and disappeared.

"Hey, wait — " Jenny called after her, but the waitress couldn't hear over the raucous shouting and laughing from the kids in the front booth. "Wow. She thought I was serious," Jenny said to Chuck.

"So did I," he grinned.

"The joke's on you," Jenny grinned back. "I don't have any money. Ha ha!"

Chuck leaped out of the booth and went running up to the front counter. "Cancel that pizza! Hey — cancel the pizza!" On his way back, he stopped at the front booth to talk to the kids from Harrison.

He's amazing, Jenny told herself. Only in school a couple of weeks, and he knows everybody! Or at least, everyone seems to know who he is. She couldn't hear what Chuck was saying, but she could hear a lot of laughing coming from the booth. He was making jokes, as usual.

When he squeezed himself back into their booth, she was surprised to see that he had a serious look on his face. "Are you busy Saturday night?" he asked, not looking at her, looking down at the red Formica table instead.

"Yes," she replied.

"That's good. Because so am I!" He exploded in laughter. It sounded forced to Jenny.

He's really disappointed, she thought. And he's covering it up by making a joke. She realized that she had just learned something important about him.

"Were you really asking me out?" she asked, a bold question for her. But she really wanted to know.

He looked down again. "Yeah."

"Well, I'd like to go out with you sometime," she said, surprised that she could say these things, that she could talk so easily to him, "but

45

I have a job. I baby-sit on Thursday and Saturday nights."

"Then how about Saturday morning?" he asked, brightening. "We could get up early and go watch cars being washed at the Kwik Wash. We could pretend it was one of those beach movies."

Jenny laughed. "I don't think so."

"I've got a better idea." He was tapping the table with his big hands, nervous, his brain in high gear. "I'll come by on Saturday night when you're baby-sitting."

"No. Bad idea," Jenny said quickly.

"Was that a yes?"

"No. It was a no."

He cupped his ear with one hand. "What? I can't hear. You said yes?"

"No. I said no," she shouted, even though she knew he could hear perfectly well.

"What time should I come by?"

"I said no. I don't want you to do that."

"Please — don't beg. I'll come. Nine o'clock too late?"

"Chuck — " She hated the peevish tone in her voice, but she couldn't help it. He was really being annoying. "Don't you know when to stop?"

"No. When? That's what I'm asking. When should I stop by?"

She got up angrily. "You're not funny."

"Who's being funny? I'm serious."

Was he deliberately trying to drive her away?

She had really enjoyed talking with him. And she was beginning to feel really attracted to him.

She thought she had been able to get past his constant joking and fooling around. But now he was deliberately being obnoxious. Why was he trying to make her angry? Because she had rejected him?

"I've got to go," she said quickly, gathering up her down jacket and backpack.

"Well, when you've gotta go, you've gotta go," he said with a shrug. "Hey — what about your pizza?"

"Put it in your memory book," she said and, pleased that she was able to think of a good parting line, turned and walked quickly from the restaurant.

Chapter 6

"Sorry I'm late," Jenny said, tossing down her backpack and pulling off her jacket. "The bus had a flat tire. Do you believe it? We were stranded. They had to call out another bus. The driver wouldn't change the tire. It's against union rules." She realized she was chattering a mile a minute, but she felt terrible being late two nights in a row.

"You should leave a little earlier," Mr. Hagen said, pulling nervously on his tie.

"It's okay," Mrs. Hagen said, giving her husband a quick frown. "You know we have plenty of time." She handed Jenny's jacket to him. He started for the coat closet, remembered the door was jammed, then jogged up the stairs to put it in the bedroom closet.

"Don't pay any attention to him," Mrs. Hagen whispered confidentially, bringing her face close to Jenny's ear. Jenny could smell her perfume. It smelled just like her mother's. "He's been very nervous. That's why I decided to get him out a couple of nights a week."

"I see," Jenny said, feeling foolish. She couldn't think of anything else to say. What was she *supposed* to say?

"I think it's the new job and the new house and everything," Mrs. Hagen continued in a low voice, looking up to the top of the stairs to make sure Mr. Hagen wasn't returning. "He's really a very sweet man, but lately he just seems to get excited about things. He worries so much more than he used to."

Jenny started to say "I see" again, but decided just to nod her head.

"I try to keep things smooth for him," Mrs. Hagen whispered. "If little things go wrong in the house while you're here, I'd really appreciate your not troubling him about them. You know what I mean."

"Sure," Jenny said. She felt flattered that Mrs. Hagen talked to her as an adult, confided in her that way.

Mr. Hagen reappeared on the stairs, and his wife quickly put a forced smile on her face. "Try to get Donny down a little early tonight," he said, picking up his gray wool overcoat from where it was draped over the bannister. "He's been looking a little pale today. He may be coming down with something."

"He looks perfectly fine to me," Mrs. Hagen said lightly. "He is naturally pale, you know, Mike."

"Not that pale," Mr. Hagen insisted. "The number where we'll be is on the pad in the kitchen."

"She knows. She knows," his wife said, pulling him by the hand. "See you later, Jenny. It shouldn't be too late. We're going to a very boring party."

"Be sure to keep the doors locked and the curtains pulled," Mr. Hagen warned as they stepped out the front door. Jenny locked the door behind them and went to look for Donny.

She found him in the den, playing with a pile of small action figures, space warriors of some kind. He dropped the figures in his hands when he saw her come in. "Let's play hide-and-seek," he said.

"Don't you say hi?" she asked, pretending to be hurt.

"Hi," he said. "Let's play hide-and-seek."

"I really don't want to," she said, stretching. "I'm kind of tired tonight. Why don't we just settle down together in the big chair and watch a tape or something?"

"I don't want to," Donny said stubbornly, sticking out his lower lip to show he planned to stick to his guns.

"Let's see if you can go an entire night without saying 'I don't want to,'" she said, sitting down on the edge of the chair cushion.

"I don't want to," he said.

I asked for that, she thought.

"I want to play hide-and-seek," he insisted,

grabbing her hand and trying to pull her up off the chair.

"Stop pulling me. I said I don't want to. I want to watch TV." She realized she was sounding as petulant as he was.

"Well, why don't we compromise?" he suggested. Suddenly he was the grown-up.

"Compromise? That's a good word." She laughed. He looked so serious.

"I learned it in school, of course," he said, talking to her as if she were six.

"Okay. What's your compromise?"

"We play hide-and-seek for just a little while!"

They both laughed. He knew he was being funny. And he knew it was impossible to say no to him. He was just too clever, too charming, too cute.

She ruffled his hair. It felt soft as feathers. "Okay. A little while," she said. "Go hide. I'll be it. But don't make it too hard, okay?"

He was already out of the room. "Count to a hundred!" he yelled from somewhere down the back hall.

Jenny counted silently to herself for a short while and then stopped. This house with its endless rooms cluttered with antique furniture, dark, empty hallways, deep closets, and dozens of hidden nooks and crannies was a great place to play hide-and-seek. Especially if you were the one who was hiding.

Why did she feel so nervous? Because she'd much rather keep Donny in sight, much rather know where he was? She was the adult here, she realized. She couldn't get into the game the way she would if she were a kid. She had to be responsible.

Did that explain her feeling of dread? Or was it something else?

She had to learn to say no to Donny, she decided. Here she was, playing this game she didn't want to play at all, just because she couldn't ever say no to him.

"Here I come, ready or not!" she shouted.

She walked quickly through the living room first, keeping her eyes low, looking under chairs and tables, even though she knew he was most likely in another room. "Here I come!" she repeated loudly, hoping he would reply somehow and give himself away.

Hearing the sound of a car out on the street, she stopped. She stood by the mantel, listening, waiting to see if the car stopped or passed by. It passed by. "Okay, I'm going to find you now!" she shouted.

She stepped into the back hallway. What was that? A giggle coming from a room she had never explored?

She entered the dark room, and her hand fumbled against the wall until she found the light switch. When she pushed it, an old, Tiffany-style lamp in a corner cast dim, orange light over the room.

Where was she? It appeared to be an extra sitting room. It was hard to tell exactly because all of the furniture — what appeared to be tall armchairs and two high-backed, facing sofas — was covered with bedsheets. A thick layer of dust had settled over everything in the room. A massive tangle of cobwebs covered the one working lamp, so thick they blocked much of the light and cast eerie shadows on the maroon wallpaper.

It looked just like a room in a haunted house movie. Jenny pictured the sheets rising up off the chairs and floating after her.

"Donny, are you hiding in here?" she called, her voice a little shaky.

A sheet over one of the tall armchairs looked a little lumpy. Had he crawled under the filthy cover to hide inside the chair?

She crept closer to the chair. Everything smelled musty and mildewed. The dust was so thick, she felt she couldn't breathe. "Are you here?" she cried.

No reply.

She crept closer.

She reached for the bottom of the sheet. She pulled it up quickly, sending a flurry of dust into the air.

No Donny.

She coughed, choking on the dry dust. "I'm getting out of here," she said aloud, and turned and walked quickly from the silent room, flicking the light switch and returning it to darkness as she left.

Still coughing, she headed into the pantry. The

shelves at floor level, she remembered, were empty. Perfect hiding places.

What was that creaking sound in the kitchen? Was that Donny? She stopped and listened. No. Maybe it wasn't coming from the kitchen. Maybe she had heard the creaking of her own shoes over the soft hallway floorboards.

She heard it again. Not footsteps. But a creaking sound. She passed by the pantry, peeked quickly into the laundry room. "Gotcha!" she yelled, running to look behind the washer-dryer. But he wasn't there.

She turned and walked to the kitchen. "Okay, Donny, here I come. I know you're in here," she called from the doorway.

Silence.

Then the creaking sound again, this time behind her.

Was it just the house groaning and creaking? The old house had dozens of different sounds that it made, all of them frightening, all of them mysterious and unexplainable.

She stopped to listen.

Was someone walking in the front hallway?

On an impulse, she turned from the kitchen and ran at full speed to the front hallway.

No. No one there.

Back to the kitchen, feeling chilled, her stomach rumbling, wishing she hadn't agreed to this game, wishing she could end it NOW! She pulled open a low cabinet door. "Gotcha!"

But he wasn't inside.

"Donny — can we quit now? I give!"

Silence.

"Can you hear me? I really don't want to play anymore."

Silence.

The creaking sound again, followed by the click of some appliance turning on.

"Donny?"

She ducked down to search under the kitchen table. Not there. She pulled open the cleaning supply closet. Not there.

"I give! You're too good a hider! I give!"

Silence.

More silence.

What if something had happened to him? What if he had picked a dangerous place to hide and had gotten himself trapped somewhere? What if he had fallen and hit his head and was lying unconscious in the basement and —

STOP!

"Donny — I give! You can come out now!"

Maybe he wasn't in the kitchen after all. Maybe he just couldn't hear her.

She was about to leave the kitchen when the door to the narrow ironing board closet flew open.

"YAAAAAIIIIII!"

She screamed in fright and tumbled to the floor as a figure came flying out at her from the tiny closet, just ahead of the ironing board, which swung down to the floor with a deafening *clang*.

"DONNY!" she cried. "You scared me to death!!"

He jumped on top of her. He was laughing and crying out triumphantly at the same time. He thought it was hilarious.

"Get off! Get off me! You really scared me!"

But her protests made him laugh even harder.

Finally he stopped laughing and helped pull her to her feet. "Your turn to hide," he said.

"Oh, no!" she cried. "The game is over."

"Scaredy cat. Chicken."

"Don't call names, Donny. It's your bedtime."

It took another forty-five minutes to get him tucked into bed. He was so excited from his hide-and-seek triumph, he couldn't calm down. She had to read three books to him, play with his stuffed animals for a while, give him a bowl of corn flakes, and bring him three glasses of apple juice before he finally caved in and agreed to try to sleep.

Feeling totally wiped out, and still a little shaky from the fright he had given her, she started down the stairs. She had brought a lot of homework, but she knew she wasn't going to look at it. She was just going to veg out in front of the tube.

She was halfway down the stairs when the phone rang. Where was the nearest phone? In the kitchen? No. The den. She ran across the living room and got to the phone on the desk in the den by the fourth ring.

It was an old-fashioned, black dial phone. She was surprised by how heavy the receiver was as she lifted it to her ear. "Hello?" She was out of breath from scrambling to the phone.

Silence.

"Hello?"

She couldn't hear anything. Maybe this old phone didn't work.

Then she heard it. Soft breathing on the other end.

Someone was definitely on the line.

"Hello?" Her voice sounded funny, high-pitched, tight. She struggled to catch her breath.

She heard the breathing, a little louder.

"Hagen residence," she said. "Who's calling?"

The breathing became louder.

Was someone trying to scare her?

"Hello? Hello?"

More loud breathing. Whoever it was was sort of groaning into the phone now.

What is going on here? she asked herself, feeling the fear begin to grow in the pit of her stomach.

Suddenly she had an idea.

A crazy idea. A stupid idea. An idea only someone with her crazy imagination would have.

Of course, she told herself, there's no way this is who I think it is on the other end of the line. But I've just got to make sure.

"Hello? What do you want?" she repeated.

The loud breathing continued.

Jenny gently placed the receiver down on the green felt blotter on the desktop. Then she ran as quickly and as silently as she could, out of the den, across the living room, up the stairs.

Of course this was insane. Truly insane.

No way. No way the breather could be him. Of all the silly ideas!

But when she got to the top landing, turned, and burst into Donny's room, there he was standing by his low, white desk, the telephone held tightly to his ear.

Chapter 7

"Donny!" Jenny screamed.

He looked up, startled. His blue eyes grew wide and he seemed to go chalk-white instantly.

She grabbed the phone from his hand roughly and held it up to her ear. There was nothing but a dial tone.

"Donny — why??"

His face twisted into a frightened frown. He looked as if he were about to cry. "You . . . scared . . . me."

"What were you doing on the phone?"

"Listening." Tears formed in his eyes, big, round ones. He rubbed them away with his little, white hands.

"Listening? What do you mean?" She looked at the phone. It had buttons for two separate lines. The phone had probably been left by the previous owner of the house. Donny could have called her on this phone.

"Just listening," he bawled. "Why did you scare me like that, Jenny?" He walked over and buried his face in her side so she wouldn't see him crying.

She had a sudden pang of guilt. "I'm sorry," she said softly, patting his head. "Don't cry. I'm sorry. Why did you call me? Were you trying to scare me?"

"No," he said, the sound muffled because his head was pressed against her waist.

"No, you weren't trying to scare me?"

"No, I didn't call."

"What? What do you mean?"

"I didn't call. Somebody else called. I was asleep. The ringing woke me up. So I picked it up to listen. But no one was talking. Then you jumped in and scared me." He started to cry loudly, pressing his head against her.

Jenny felt terrible. Was he telling the truth?

Of course he was. How could she have suspected a six-year-old child? How could she have suspected Donny? Once again, her stupid imagination had gotten her into trouble.

She hugged him and apologized and did her best to comfort him. Then she led him back to his bed and tucked him in. "Now tell me the story," he said.

"No, Donny. It's way too late. And I really don't think I could tell it right now."

"But you promised!" he whined. He was so tired, he could barely keep his eyes open. "You promised and you forgot."

"Next time I'll tell it twice," she said, smoothing the feathery blond hair off his forehead. "I just can't tonight, Donny. I'm sorry. I'm really sorry."

He was too sleepy to protest any more. She tiptoed out of the room, feeling guilty, feeling like a monster, telling herself she'd never suspect him of anything ever again.

It hadn't even sounded like a child's breathing. What had made her think it was Donny in the first place?

And the furious way she had leaped at him and grabbed the phone out of his hand! She'd never forgive herself.

I was just scared, that's all, she argued with herself.

Don't make excuses, Jenny. You wanted the caller to be a six-year-old because then you wouldn't have to be afraid, then you'd be in control.

But he looked so guilty when I walked into his room. The way he went pale like that, as if he knew he'd just been caught doing something terrible.

She didn't have any more time to argue with herself. As she reached the bottom of the stairs, she hung up the phone. It rang almost immediately.

The sound sent a chill down her back. She stood frozen in the front hallway, her eyes closed, wishing it away, wishing it to stop.

But it rang again. And again. I'm just not going to answer it, she told herself. But then she realized the ringing would wake up Donny again.

And what if it wasn't the breather calling back? What if it was a call for Mr. or Mrs. Hagen?

She took a deep breath, ran to the den, and picked up the phone. "Hello?"

Silence.

"Hello?"

"Hi, Babes."

The voice was a hoarse whisper.

"Who is this?" Jenny demanded.

"Hi, Babes. Are you all alone?" She couldn't tell if it was a man or a boy.

"What do you want?" She tried not to sound frightened, but she couldn't help it.

"Are you all alone in that big house? Well, don't worry. Company's coming."

"Listen, you — "

She heard a soft click at the other end.

Chapter 8

Jenny stared at the heavy receiver in her hand and listened to the drone of the dial tone until her heart stopped pounding. Her hand was trembling. Her throat felt tight and dry.

Someone was trying to scare her — and was doing a pretty good job of it!

Someone knew she was there. Someone knew she was alone.

Someone knew her.

Or did they?

Everyone knew about weirdos who got their kicks by making sick phone calls to strangers. Maybe this was some creep picking phone numbers at random, some guy going through the phone book, seeing who he could upset, who he could get a reaction from.

Or maybe it was a kid. Some guy from school, trying to be funny.

Trying to be funny?

Chuck?

Would Chuck do something like that?

No. Of course not. He was a joker, a goof. Everything he did was good-natured. Or was it? She didn't really know Chuck that well. Actually, she didn't know Chuck at all.

She suddenly remembered their conversation at the Pizza Oven, how Chuck's mood had suddenly changed after she told him she couldn't go out with him on Saturday night. He hadn't seemed so good-natured then. In fact, he was downright obnoxious. It was as if he had turned against her, as if he had tried to make her angry.

But perhaps he was just disappointed, just hurt that she had turned him down, and that she hadn't wanted him to drop by the Hagens' when she was baby-sitting.

That didn't mean he was capable of making those frightening calls. That didn't mean he would do such a disgusting, sick thing.

She refused to believe it was Chuck.

But then, who? Someone nearby? Someone in the neighborhood? Someone who had been watching the house, had seen her arrive, had seen the Hagens leave?

Was there someone out there who really was preparing to harm her?

"Are you all alone?" he had whispered. *"Are you all alone in that big house?"*

He knew where she was. He knew she was alone.

"Don't worry — company's coming!"

"Company's coming!"

When? Tonight?

The neighbor!

What was his name? Willers. Willers would know she was there. Willers would know she was alone.

Of course.

That gravelly voice. That hoarse whisper.

Willers was so creepy, the way he stared at her, the way he looked her up and down.

It had to be Willers.

She grabbed the phone to call the police. Then she took her hand away.

She had never called the police before. She had only seen it done in movies and on TV. People in real life didn't call the police, did they?

They did if they were frightened. They did if someone was threatening them, someone who lived right next door.

But would they believe her? What would they say?

"Oh, Jenny," she imagined the policeman's bored reply, "we all know about your wild imagination. These calls are all in your mind. Please don't bother us. We have real work to do."

Even if they believed her, what would they do? They probably had dozens of weird calls reported every night. What could they do about it? Send someone out to hold her hand until the Hagens returned home?

"Are you all alone? Don't worry, company's coming!"

I don't care, she thought. I'm calling the police.

She reached for the phone again, and as she did, it seemed to explode in her hand.

"YAAAAIII!" she screamed and jumped a mile in the air.

But it wasn't exploding. It was only ringing. Again.

"Oh, no," she said aloud. "Please — leave me alone."

Her hand reached out and gripped the receiver, but she didn't pick it up. She could feel each ring vibrating up her arm. Finally she picked it up just to stop the noise.

"Hello?" Her voice sounded strange to her, high and frightened.

"Hi, Jenny. Just wanted to see how you're doing."

"Mr. Hagen?"

"Right. Everything okay? I guess you were far from the phone. It rang so many times, I was a little worried."

"I . . . uh . . . was in the bathroom. Sorry."

Was that the best excuse she could think of? It didn't matter. It was good enough.

She was very relieved to hear his voice.

"Donny okay? Did you get him to bed early?"

"Well . . . pretty early. He's fine. No problem."

"Sometimes he takes advantage of his sitters and stays up really late. He looks like an angel, but he can be a real devil."

Did he really mean that? Was Donny really capable of being evil?

Of course not. Have you lost your mind entirely, Jenny? Just calm down. Take a deep breath and calm yourself down.

"No. He was no trouble. Really." Mr. Hagen

certainly is a nervous parent, she thought. She looked at her watch. He'd only been away two and a half hours. Why was he calling?

"Is he sleeping okay? Sometimes he throws off his covers and then he gets cold in the middle of the night."

"I checked him once. He was fine," she said. "I'll go up and check again."

"Good. Sounds like everything is under control. We won't be too late. Another hour or two. You have the number here, right?"

"Yes. I have it."

Should she tell him about the calls? She was so tempted to tell him! But no. She held herself back. He's so nervous, he'd probably call out the FBI, the CIA, and the National Guard! she told herself. And Mrs. Hagen asked me not to upset him.

"Okay, Jenny. 'Bye. Hope you don't mind my checking in like this."

"No. I'm glad. I mean . . . it's okay. Everything's fine."

"Good. Help yourself to anything in the kitchen. And keep the doors locked."

Don't worry. "Yes, I will. Thanks."

Finally he hung up. Despite her fear, Jenny had to smile. Mr. Hagen looked so big and macho, but he was such a Nervous Nellie. He was sweet, though. It was sweet the way he worried about Donny.

She realized she felt better after talking with him. She decided she wouldn't call the police after all. They would probably only take down the information and then forget about it. What else could they do?

She felt edgy, restless. She paced back and forth in the living room for a while, but the creaking floor and the ticking of the grandfather's clock made her even more nervous. She went back to the den and pulled her government textbook from her backpack. But there was no way she could concentrate on the separation of powers tonight.

She shoved the book back into the backpack, paced back and forth in the small den for a few minutes, then decided to get a Coke in the kitchen. Crossing the living room again, a framed photograph on an end table by the worn sofa caught her eye. It was a color portrait of Donny. She had never noticed it before.

She walked to the end table and picked up the photo to examine it more closely. "He must have been only two or three when this was taken," she thought. Then her mouth dropped open in surprise.

The child in the photo looked a lot like Donny, had the same blue eyes, the same white-blond hair — but it wasn't Donny. For one thing, this child had a pink ribbon in its hair. And was wearing a green corduroy jumper. This child was a girl.

Jenny stared at the photo. The child was so beautiful, it was hard to take her eyes off her. "Donny has a sister," Jenny told herself. "But where?"

Then she realized what the horrible truth must be.

"Donny *had* a sister."

She dropped the photograph onto the desk and looked away. She couldn't bear to look at it any longer.

This explained a lot. It certainly explained why Mr. Hagen was so nervous and worried about Donny. The poor man. The poor family. It probably also explained why Mr. Hagen had changed jobs, why they had moved to this neighborhood on the far edge of town.

The room suddenly seemed stuffy and hot. Jenny went to the window and pulled back the heavy, crushed-velvet drapes. She peered out through the frost-stained glass.

It was cool by the window. The cold wind seeped in through the cracked glass. Outside, the wind swirled, whistling loudly, shaking the leafless trees, making them clatter like dry, brittle skeletons.

The moon was full, a gold coin in a pink-gray sky. On the radio, they had said it could snow. The pink sky meant that snow clouds hovered above. The strange lighting gave the ground an unreal look, made everything clearer and brighter than real life.

What was that in the front yard? Jenny squinted through the glass.

Were they squirrels? The squirrels seemed to be holding paws. There were four or five of them, dancing in a circle, holding onto each other, twirling faster and faster, first in one direction, then the other.

No.

That's not right.

Jenny realized they weren't squirrels. They were leaves, blowing round and round in the swirling winds.

Stop doing that, girl, she scolded herself. They'll lock you up if you keep seeing things.

She squinted again, trying to make the leaves turn back into squirrels. It was such a wonderful, comical scene. But the wind had changed. The leaves had blown away. She couldn't bring it back.

She had a sudden chill. The face of the little girl in the picture, Donny's sister, floated back into her mind. She tried to blink it away.

Taking a step back, she started to pull the drapes into place. But something else outside caught her eye.

Was there a car parked at the curb in front of the house?

No. It was probably a tree stump. She started to scold herself again for seeing what wasn't there. But no matter how hard she squinted, she couldn't make the small, black car turn into a tree stump.

It was a car. She wasn't imagining it.

And that shadow in the front seat. . . .

The shadow moved.

There was a man sitting in the car.

Why? What was he doing there? Was he

watching her? Was he waiting for . . . for what??

"Don't worry, company's coming!"

"Company's coming!"

Jenny yanked the drapes shut and went one more time to make sure the doors were locked.

Chapter 9

"Here. Put some more syrup on those."

Mrs. Jeffers leaned over Jenny and poured the thick, brown syrup onto the stack of pancakes.

"Don't, Mom. Stop!" Jenny pushed her mother's arm away. They had the same argument every Sunday morning. "That's too much. You want me to weigh three hundred pounds?"

"No, I don't," Mrs. Jeffers sat down across from Jenny at the small kitchen table. "But I would like you to put a little meat on those bones."

"Mom, really," Jenny said, a mouthful of soft, warm pancakes making it hard to talk. She swallowed. Delicious! "I'm going to be skinny like you my whole life. Skinny and flat-chested. It's hereditary."

Her mother smiled. She never laughed. "You don't have to blame me for everything." She raised a hand to brush a wisp of hair from over her eye. Jenny was surprised to see that she had a few gray hairs. She had never noticed them before.

Suddenly her mother looked very tired to her. Maybe she'd looked that way for a long time. Jenny realized she seldom really looked at her mother at all. She wondered if her mother looked this sad and tired down at the office, too. A picture flashed into her mind of her mother at the law office where she worked, laughing and joking with the other legal secretaries, running around energetically, suddenly tap dancing on the top of a desk, leaping off it into the arms of one of the lawyers.

"More orange juice?" her mother asked, yawning.

"Mom, I still have a full glass."

"Oh. Sorry." Mrs. Jeffers took a small bite of the single pancake on her plate. "Chilly in here, isn't it?" She pulled her cotton robe around her tighter. "When did you get in last night?"

"Late. About one, I guess."

"Mr. Hagen drove you home?"

"Yes. He's such a worrier. He'd never let me take the bus home."

"I should hope not." The wisp of hair fell down over her eye again. This time, she left it there. She took another nibble of the pancake. "I'm glad he's a worrier. I worry, too. They live so far away. And with these awful news stories. . . ."

"Yeah, I know." Jenny didn't feel like telling her there was more to worry about than just the distance.

"How come you're not eating?"

"Mom, I am, too. You piled on a dozen pancakes here. I'm not Arnold Schwarzenegger, you know!" She didn't mean to sound so shrill. She was very tired, she realized.

"Okay, okay."

They ate in silence for a few minutes. Then Jenny looked up to see that her mother had a strange smile on her face. "What's that smile for?" she asked, wiping syrup off her upper lip with her napkin.

"You've been keeping something from me, haven't you."

What? Did she know about what happened at the Hagens? About the frightening phone calls? No. If that's what she meant, she wouldn't be smiling like that.

"Come on, Jenny, 'fess up. You know it isn't nice to keep secrets from your loving mother."

Jenny laughed. It wasn't like her mother to tease her like this. She usually just said what she meant. "What are you talking about?"

"You know. I'm talking about Chuck."

"Chuck?!"

"Don't act so dumb. That's his name, right? Chuck Quinn?"

"Yes. I know a guy named Chuck Quinn, but — "

"You're blushing." Her mother's smile grew wider.

"I am not," Jenny insisted. "Stop teasing me, Mother. I really don't like it. What about Chuck? Did he call you?"

"You didn't tell me there was a boy interested in you. Did he stop by when you were baby-sitting last night? I really don't approve of that."

"No, he didn't," Jenny said, her mind spinning. "Did Chuck call you? Did he?"

"Yes." Her mother seemed surprised by Jenny's reaction. "He called last night. About seven-thirty. He said he needed your phone number and address. You know, at the Hagens. I was a little reluctant to give it to him, but he seemed very polite, and he said you had given it to him already, but he had lost it."

"That's not true," Jenny said.

"Uh-oh. Did I do something wrong?" Her mother tightened her hands into little fists, the way she always did when she was upset.

"No. You didn't do anything wrong." No point in getting her mother all worked up, Jenny thought.

"He didn't call you?"

"No."

Maybe he did. Jenny had a heavy feeling in the pit of her stomach, and she knew it wasn't from the pancakes.

Maybe he did.

Chuck got the phone number from my mom. Then he called and tried to frighten me with his disgusting breathing and horrible threats.

She had a feeling all along that it had been Chuck. There was obviously something wrong with him. He was dangerous. He was out of control. He had seemed out of control to her in school, always joking, always trying to trick the teachers, always trying to be the center of attention.

Everyone thought he was so funny. But he wasn't funny. He was sick.

Her mother thought it was cute that a boy was interested in her. If only she knew why he was interested. He was only interested in making her his victim!

And now he not only had the Hagens' phone number; he had the address, too.

That must have been him, sitting in that little car in front of the house. Waiting there, waiting for me, his victim, to come out, waiting for me to —

No. Wait.

There she went again, letting her imagination run wild. She realized she was being terribly unfair, jumping to conclusions that might not be true. That couldn't be true!

Just because Chuck had the phone number didn't mean that he was the one who had called — did it?

She had no right to accuse him.

She should give him the benefit of the doubt, right? He didn't seem like such a bad guy, after all. In fact, he was kind of sweet. He was funny. He was a class clown. He wasn't evil.

Or was he?

"You look terribly worried. If I did anything wrong. . . ." Mrs. Jeffers interrupted Jenny's confused thoughts.

Jenny forced a smile. "No. I'm sorry, Mom. I

was thinking about something else. I'm really tired, that's all. Everything's fine. Chuck's really a nice boy. He's new. He just moved to Harrison a few weeks ago."

"You do look tired," her mother said.

"What would you think if I quit my baby-sitting job?" Jenny asked suddenly. The idea popped into her head, and she said it. She regretted it immediately as soon as she saw the disappointed look on her mother's face.

"Is it really too much for you?"

"Well, no. . . ."

"Then I really think you should stick with it, Jen. It's such a bad habit, not sticking with things. You just started, you know. You'll get used to the routine."

"I know, but — "

"And we really can use the money you're making. The Hagens are so generous. Christmas will be here before you know it, and — "

"You're right, Mom. It was a stupid idea. I don't know why I said it."

I do know why I said it, Jenny thought as she carried her breakfast dishes to the sink. I said it because I want to run away. Mom's right. I always try to run away from everything. Well, this time I'm going to surprise everyone — including myself. I'm not going to run away, not from the baby-sitting job, and not from Chuck.

"See you later, Mom. I'm meeting Laura at the mall." She gave her mom a quick kiss on the forehead and headed out the kitchen door.

"Don't worry so much about things," her

mother called after her. "Everything will be fine."

I hope you're right, Jenny thought, searching the coat closet for her down jacket. I sure hope you're right.

"It couldn't be Chuck," Laura said. "He's a teddy bear!"

"Yeah, you're right," Jenny said.

"How could you accuse someone with that little boy face and those freckles? No way!" Laura continued. She picked up a pack of bright magenta press-on fingernails. "What do you think? You just press these on, and instant cool!"

"Instant weird, you mean," Jenny said, grabbing the package from Laura's hand and examining the nails carefully. "Really gross."

"I thought I'd surprise Bob Tanner tonight with something a little different."

"Get real. You wouldn't wear these things, would you?"

Laura shrugged. "I guess not." They walked out of Cosmetics Plus, past Earring World. "Maybe I'll go in and get my nose pierced."

"You can't," Jenny said, pulling her past the store. "You need a parent's permission if you're under eighteen."

"How do you know?"

"Ellen Sappers tried to get her ears pierced in three stores a few weeks ago, and they wouldn't do it without a note from her mother."

"Did she get the note?"

"No way. Ellen said that if her mother approved of it, she didn't want to do it."

"Let's go into Sock City," Jenny said. "I like to look at socks."

"You're definitely in a weird mood," Laura said, following her into the narrow store.

"So did you really break up with Eugene?"

"Look at these, Jenny. Who would wear socks with little pink pigs on them?"

"I have a pair just like those. Did you break up with Eugene?"

"Kind of."

"What do you mean?"

"I mean I stood him up."

"You just didn't show up for your date last night?"

"I thought it was kinder than telling him I'm sick of him. I didn't really want to hurt him."

"Laura, I don't believe you!"

Laura grabbed Jenny's arm. "You won't believe this, either! Look who's here!"

Jenny looked to where her friend was gesturing. There was Chuck, rummaging through a basket of sweat socks in the back of the store.

"Quick, Laura — move. Let's get out of here before he sees us." She shoved Laura toward the door.

"Too late," Laura said.

"Hi!" Chuck dropped the socks in his hand, and came jogging over. "We've got to stop meeting like this." He grinned at Jenny, a goofy Huck Finn grin.

"What are *you* doing here?" Laura asked.

"Hey, I wear socks, you know. I have a right to come in here, too."

Laura laughed. "I didn't mean it like that."

Jenny backed away without realizing it. She really didn't want to talk to Chuck. She needed time to think, time to figure out what she felt about him.

"How was the baby-sitting?" he asked her, picking up the pig socks and examining them. "Everything go okay?"

He's not looking me in the eye, Jenny realized. He's pretending to look closely at the socks instead. He *can't* look me in the eye.

"It was okay," she said quickly.

"I like these socks," Chuck said, waving them in front of him. "They'll look nice with my polka-dot 501s!"

Laura laughed. Jenny smiled briefly. He still wasn't looking at her.

"Are you guilty, Chuck?" she wanted to ask. "Are you feeling a little guilty about the calls you made last night?"

Finally he turned to her with a serious look on his face. He put a big hand on the shoulder of her jacket. "Listen, Jenny . . . uh . . . I want to apologize."

She stared back at him. She couldn't speak. Was he really going to admit it? How could he admit doing such a horrible thing?

"Apologize?" she finally managed to say.

"Should I leave?" Laura asked, grinning, looking as if leaving was the last thing on her mind.

"Apologize for what?" Jenny asked, ignoring Laura, keeping her voice low and steady.

"For being so obnoxious Friday afternoon. At the Pizza Oven. I really shouldn't have given you such a hard time about not wanting me to come by while you were baby-sitting."

"Oh. I mean . . . that's okay."

"Oh? It *is* okay? Great! I'll be there Thursday night!"

All three of them laughed.

Chuck pulled one of the pig socks down over his hand and made a hand puppet out of it. "Hi, girls," he made the sock say in a high, squeaky voice. "Want a sock in the nose?"

The store manager, a short, bald man with a sour expression, cleared his throat and shook his head at Chuck.

"We socks can all talk, but he won't let us!" Chuck made the sock say. "That's because he's a heel!"

"Are you buying those socks?" the manager barked.

"Do you take Confederate money?" Chuck asked, reaching for his wallet.

The manager just scowled.

"Then we're leaving!" Chuck told him. "It doesn't fit, anyway. It's tight around the knuckles." He pulled off the sock and dropped it back onto the shelf. "Let's go, girls."

The three of them held their breaths until they were several yards from the store. Then they burst out laughing.

"Hey — look what's at the theater!" Chuck

cried, pointing at the sign in front of the mall movie theater. "A clay animation festival! Neat! Come on — let's go!"

"What? We can't!" Jenny protested.

"Why not?" Chuck looked surprised.

"Well . . . uh . . . I don't know!" Jenny couldn't think of any reasons.

"I can't," Laura said, looking at her pink-and-black Swatch. "I promised my mom I'd be home. But you two go on without me." She gave Jenny a meaningful look.

"Laura — "

"Okay. Come on, Jenny," Chuck said eagerly. "I'll even treat."

"No, I — " Jenny looked imploringly at Laura for some help, but Laura was ignoring her plea.

"Have a great time," Laura said. She obviously thought Jenny and Chuck would make a great couple and was doing her best to see that they became a couple despite Jenny's misgivings.

She really likes bullying people, Jenny thought. Do all short people like to push people around?

Of course, Laura wouldn't see it that way. Laura would see it as only trying to help. She gave Jenny and Chuck a wave and, looking very pleased with herself, headed past the fountain and toward the exit.

"Come on. It just started," Chuck said, taking Jenny's hand. He smiled at her, and blushed.

He's actually very shy, she realized. Maybe that's why he wasn't looking me in the eye before.

"Okay," she said, and hurried with him up to the window of the box office.

"Two," he told the girl behind the glass.

Jenny smiled. She liked being part of a two. And she liked being with Chuck.

If only she knew the answer to one question. . . . Was he the one? Was he the one who called to frighten her the night before?

Chapter 10

"Tell me another story."

"No. Come on, Donny. I've already told you a really long one. It's time for you to go to sleep. Look at the clock on your dresser. It says nine-thirty."

"So?"

"So, it's bedtime."

Jenny had played three games of Chutes & Ladders with him and an endless card game called Uno, and now she was sitting on the edge of his bed, trying to coax him to go to sleep.

"A short story. Very short?"

"No deals. Bedtime is bedtime. Give me a break. I need some time to myself."

"No!" He made an angry face and tossed a stuffed bear across the room.

Jenny nearly laughed. It was funny to see someone who looked so angelic trying to act bad.

He heaved another stuffed animal across the room. It hit the wall and slid to the floor. "Are you gonna tell me another story or not?" he demanded, sticking out his lower lip like a tough guy.

"Not," Jenny said, beginning to lose patience. She knew he was just testing her, seeing how far he could push her around.

"You know, I know some bad words," he said. It wasn't a threat. It was a secret he was sharing with her. "Want to hear some?" He gave her a conspiratorial smile.

"Not tonight," she said wearily. "Please. It's getting really late. Don't make me get angry."

He climbed beside her on the bed and sat real close. She could feel the heat radiating off his thin body. He was always as warm as a furnace. "What do you do when you get angry?" He was testing her now.

She had to smile. "When I get angry, I . . . turn into a WEREWOLF!" She roared at him like an angry beast.

He laughed. "Okay. Get angry. I want to see."

She jumped up from the bed and leaned over him, putting her hands on his tiny shoulders. "You wouldn't like it if I got all hairy and grew fangs."

"Sure, I would. Do it. Do it!" He pulled away from her, stood up, and began jumping up and down, using his bed as a trampoline.

It took another half an hour to get him tucked in. He was going out of his way to be difficult, but it was so hard to get angry at someone that cute. Girls had better watch out for him in a few years! Jenny told herself, walking down the stairs.

She entered the den and picked up her backpack. She had come better prepared tonight with things to keep her entertained and keep her mind off the creepiness of the old house and how alone she was. Slipping her Walkman over her ears, she shuffled through the tapes she had brought, pushed a new Bangles cassette in, and turned up the volume. Then she pulled out her government textbook and searched for the pages she had to read.

The loud music made it easier to study. It shut out the rest of the world and forced her to concentrate harder on the words. At least, that was Jenny's theory.

Suddenly she pulled off the headphones and listened.

Was that Donny calling?

Was the phone ringing?

No. The house was silent except for the constant clicking of the grandfather clock in the living room.

Maybe the Walkman was a bad idea, she decided. Donny was still awake upstairs. He might call her for some reason, and she wouldn't be able to hear him. He might come to the edge of the stairs when she didn't respond to his calls. He might start down the stairs. He might fall.

He might fall and — stop! Stop dreaming up fresh worries!

She clicked off the Walkman, folded up the headphones, and replaced it in her backpack. I'm on duty, she reminded herself. I've got to remember, got to stay alert, got to stay at attention, like a soldier on guard duty.

And what was the penalty for a soldier who fell asleep on guard duty? Instant death! Hadn't she seen that in some movie? Or did she make it up?

She tried reading more about separation of powers in her government book, but it was hard to concentrate without the music. Suddenly feeling thirsty, she turned the textbook over and placed it on the table, climbed out of the low leather chair, and walked to the kitchen.

All of the lights were on in the living room, making it a lot brighter and less depressing than on the other nights. It was a still night outside, and so the shutter didn't bang and the wind didn't howl, and in general the atmosphere was a lot less threatening.

"If only I could do something about that awful clock," she told herself. For a brief moment, she was tempted to go over to it, grab the pendulum, and hold onto it until she had stopped the ticking forever.

She walked into the kitchen, switched on the lights, and headed to the refrigerator for a Coke. She found herself suddenly thinking about Chuck. They had had such a nice time together on Sunday. He really was a lot of fun to be with, not at all goofy and hard to talk to, the way she had imagined. He was very funny and entertaining, his mind was so quick, but he could also stop the jokes when he wanted to. During those times he was shy, and Jenny thought, even cuter.

He had come over to her house to study on Tuesday night. Jenny's mom had thought he was really terrific, too. Sure, he did some pretty gross things with a bunch of bananas he found on their kitchen table — but he wouldn't be Chuck if he didn't clown around some of the time.

If only . . . if only there weren't that one question she had about him, nagging at the back of her mind, keeping her from really being able to feel close to Chuck. If only she knew. . . .

She almost asked him once during their study date, almost asked him point-blank if he had made those frightening calls. But she stopped. She couldn't. If he said yes, it would ruin everything. And if he said no — then *she* would have ruined everything. He would never forgive her for accusing him. He'd have every right never to speak to her again.

And so she had pushed it out of her mind. At least she had tried to. And she found herself liking him more and more.

She snapped open the Coke and took a sip from the can. When the phone rang, she thought it must be Chuck. She had told him in school that afternoon that he could call.

She picked up the receiver of the kitchen wall phone and said brightly, "Hello. Hagen residence."

"Hi, Babes."

The gruff, whispered voice.

She gasped. Her bright mood vanished, replaced by the cold dread she had felt on Saturday night. She could feel her muscles grow tense. Her heart began to pound. She gripped the bright red phone receiver so tightly her hand began to ache.

"Hi, Babes. Are you all alone?"

She didn't say anything.

She wanted to shout, to scream at this creep, to slam the phone down as hard as she could. But she didn't say anything, and she didn't move. It was as if the whispered words had paralyzed her, frozen her with their menace.

"Don't be sad. I'll be there soon. Then the fun will really begin."

Was it Chuck?

She couldn't tell. It might be. No. It couldn't be.

"I'm . . . calling the police," she finally managed to say. She didn't recognize her high, tight voice. It was as if someone else was speaking, as if this was happening to someone else.

"See you soon, Babes."

There was a CLICK at the other end.

She stood there for a long while, receiver pressed to her ear, listening to the steady hum of the dial tone. The sound was soothing somehow. It meant that the whispered threats were over.

Jenny jammed the receiver back onto the wall, then ran to the back door and made sure it was locked.

Now what?

Now what?

She was pacing back and forth the length of the kitchen without realizing it. She picked up the can of Coke, took a long swig to moisten her achingly dry throat, then carried the can with her as she paced.

Now what?

Now what?

Her hands were ice-cold. Her muscles all felt tight and knotted. She heard a car door slam somewhere down the street.

"I'll be there soon. Then the fun will really begin."

She stopped pacing and listened.

Silence.

She knew what she had to do. She picked up the phone and pushed O. After three rings, a husky woman's voice said, "Operator."

"Please. Put me through to the police." It was all unreal. None of this was happening. What was she going to say? What were *they* going to say?

"Do you want the town police or the village police?"

"What? Oh. I don't know. I mean — "

"Are you in Harrison, or are you in the village?" The woman was trying to be helpful. But her calm, steady tone was driving Jenny crazy. Didn't she realize that Jenny was frightened? Why couldn't she sound frightened and upset, too?

"I — I'm not sure. I'm in the Old Village. Edgetown Lane. Off Millertown."

"Then you probably want the village police."

Probably?? "Oh. Thank you."

"You can dial them directly. The number is 066-1919."

"What? Dial them? Can't you — What was the number again?"

The operator repeated the number, then clicked off.

Jenny pushed the number, got it wrong the first time, then pushed it again.

"Village police, Officer Mertz."

"Hello, Mr. Mertz. I mean — Officer — "

"Can I help you?"

"I — I want to report some calls."

"You want to make some calls?"

"No. I've been getting these calls." *Calm down, Jenny. Calm down. You're not going to make any sense at all if you don't lower your voice and speak more clearly, more slowly.*

"Is this a matter for the phone company?"

"No. I'm sorry. I've been getting these calls, threatening calls."

"Someone is threatening you?"

"Yes. On the phone. Whispering."

"Where are you calling from?"

"Edgetown Lane. 142 Edgetown. Off Millertown."

"Your name?"

"I'm Jenny Jeffers. But I don't live here. I mean, it's not my house. I'm the baby-sitter."

"Have you heard any strange sounds in the house or outside? Seen any unfamiliar cars? Any sign of anyone outside?"

"Yes. I don't know. I mean, no. Not tonight. Just the calls."

"I see." He seemed to be writing everything down. "Do you think this could be a friend of yours, maybe someone from school, someone pulling a prank?"

"I don't know. I don't think so. Are you going to send someone out to investigate?"

"Investigate what? We can't investigate phone calls."

"Oh. I guess you're right. I just — "

"Is there someone you could call to come stay with you? Someone you trust?"

"Well . . . no. My mother isn't home tonight. Uh . . . I could call a girlfriend, maybe."

"It might help make you feel better. Chances are, it's just a phone creep. These guys never go outdoors. They stay in, making charming threats, getting their kicks by frightening people. But they seldom show up at the door."

"That's good."

"Normally, I'd tell you not to worry. But because of the baby-sitter attacks, we have to take this seriously. I'm going to give you a different phone number. This is the number of Lieutenant Ferris from the town police. This type of thing is sort of his department." He gave Jenny Lieutenant Ferris's phone number. She wrote it down quickly on a sheet of paper towel she tore off the rack over the sink.

"Got it," she said. "I should call him — "

"If you get any more threats. Or if you hear anything unusual, or see anything unusual. Just call that number. Ferris will be there. He's the man who can help you. But as I say, these phone creeps seldom leave their princess phones."

"Thanks, officer. Thanks for your help."

"Just doing my job."

Jenny replaced the receiver and stood staring at the number she had written on the paper towel. Then she folded it carefully and pushed it into her jeans pocket.

She was feeling a little better. At least, her heart had stopped pounding like a bass drum and her neck muscles weren't so tense and tight. She took a long swig of the Coke and started toward the den with it.

Passing the stairs in the front hallway, she suddenly remembered Donny. She turned and headed up the stairs to check on him. She tiptoed into his room to find him sleeping lightly with his eyes open. He looked as if he were staring right at her, even though he was asleep.

How do kids do that? she wondered. It looks so strange.

She was starting to feel a lot more normal as she headed back down the stairs. Calling the police had helped a lot. That officer had been so calm and reassuring. And it made her feel good to have a special phone number to call in an emergency.

"These guys never go out," the policeman had told her. "They never show up at your door."

She was halfway across the living room when she heard the loud knocking.

She jumped. Her heart seemed to skip a beat.

No, she thought. That's the loose shutter banging against the house.

But it couldn't be. There was no wind.

She heard it again. Four hard raps. Someone was knocking on the front door.

She ran to the door. "Who's there?" she called.

No reply.

If only there were a chain on the door. If only there were a peephole.

Four loud knocks.

"Who is it?"

Silence.

An idea flashed into her head. The living room window. Maybe she could see the front porch from the living room window. Maybe she could see who it was from there.

Three more knocks.

She ran into the living room, tripping over a tear in the worn carpet. She fell, hitting her left knee hard. Pain throbbed up her leg. She pulled herself to her feet. She hobbled the rest of the way. Her knee throbbed, but it was okay.

She pulled back the heavy drapes. Light from the porch light cast a yellow glow over the front yard.

Suddenly someone leaped up on the other side of the glass, as if being shot up from under the ground.

"YAAAAAIII!"

The scream ripped from Jenny's throat as she saw the hideous, deformed figure staring back at her, his twisted face pressed menacingly against the windowpane.

Chapter 11

No. This has to be a nightmare, Jenny thought.

This person — this creature — can't be real.

Then she realized it was a mask. It was someone in a monster mask, with enormous rubber fangs, huge bloodshot eyes that popped out two inches from their bloody sockets, and long tangles of red vinyl hair that shot straight up in the air.

"Don't worry. Company's coming."

"I'll be there soon. Then the fun will really begin."

Jenny reached into her jeans pocket for the piece of paper with the policeman's number on it. Where had she put it? She had written the number on a paper towel and put it — Here it is.

But would she have time to call?

Would the police be able to get there in time before this creep . . . before he. . . .

He pulled off the mask.

"CHUCK!!" Jenny screamed. "Chuck — how could you?? Why??"

"Gotcha! he called through the window glass. He tossed the hideous mask high in the air and, laughing like a lunatic, leaped up after it. Then he did a cartwheel on the grass. Still laughing jubilantly over his triumphant joke, he walked back to the window and pressed his nose against the glass.

Jenny's terror quickly turned to fury. She slammed the drapes shut and strode angrily to the front door, her hands still shaking as she turned the lock and pulled open the door.

Chuck was waiting for her on the porch, grinning like he'd just won the World Series of Practical Jokes, turning the disgusting mask over and over in his hands. "I *knew* you'd come to the window," he laughed. "You should've seen your face!"

"Go away, you dork!" Jenny screamed. "Get lost! I mean it!"

He didn't seem to hear her. Or maybe he didn't realize she was completely serious. "I gotcha. I really gotcha. Whoa! That was incredible!"

"You're not funny. You're sick! You scared me to death." She started to slam the door, but he shoved his foot into the opening.

She felt a stab of renewed fear. He had moved so quickly, so deftly to block the door, as if he had done it before. She had the sudden realization that maybe he had come to harm her. Maybe he was the whispered voice on the phone. Maybe he truly was dangerous.

She didn't really know him, after all.

No one did.

"Move away, Chuck. I don't want to see you. I'm — "

"You look cute when you're scared."

Was he trying to make her more scared?

"Go away! I really mean it. I'm furious at you. You're not funny. Stop smiling at me like that!"

The smile faded slowly. "Come on, Jenny — "

"No."

"It's cold out here. Just let me come in for a few minutes."

"No. Go away."

He gave her a pleading, little-boy look. "Please? I'll let you try on the mask!" More high-pitched laughing. He really thought he was a riot.

"I'm serious, Chuck. Move your foot. I don't want to see you. You had no right to scare me like that."

He finally began to realize that she meant what she said. He let the mask fall to the porch floor and shrugged. "Sorry."

"Apology not accepted," she said, pushing on the door. "Good night."

"You're right, Jenny. It was stupid. I don't know what I was thinking of. I just wanted to surprise you, I guess."

"Surprise me?! Well, you did a great job, Ace!"

A cold burst of wind caught them both by surprise. They heard a crash somewhere down the street, a garbage can being knocked over, the lid rattling down the street.

"I'm really freezing, Jenny," he wrapped his arms around himself. She saw for the first time that he had no coat, only a gray sweatshirt. He looked really cold, and really apologetic. And really cute, hugging himself like that, his eyes pleading with her like a little boy begging for a cookie. "Can't I come in?"

"I guess. Just for a second. Hurry." She backed away, and he eagerly stepped into the narrow hallway, shivering, still hugging himself.

"You can't stay long. The Hagens may be home soon. Mr. Hagen is so nervous. He'd kill me if he found a boy here with me."

He followed her into the living room. "Wow! What a dump!"

"They're planning to redo it all. They just moved in."

"This room is huge. Great place to party!"

She spun around angrily. "Stop talking like that. This is my job."

He looked hurt. "Sorry. I'm sorry. Sorry. Sorry. Sorry."

She started to say something, but she heard footsteps running down the stairs. Donny, in his G.I. Joe pajamas, burst into the room, one cheek bright red from where he'd been sleeping on it. "Who's he?" he demanded, pointing at Chuck.

"He's my friend Chuck," Jenny said quickly, giving Chuck an annoyed look. She really didn't want Donny to know she'd had a visitor. Donny was certain to tell his parents.

"Hi, Donny," Chuck said, giving him a big, friendly grin.

"How'd you know my name?" Donny asked suspiciously.

"Just took a lucky guess," Chuck said, still grinning.

Donny thought that was funny.

"Donny, what are you doing up?" Jenny demanded.

Donny ignored her question. He pointed to the mask in Chuck's hand. "What's that?"

"A monster mask." Chuck held it up so he could see it. "Want to try it on?"

"Yeah!" Donny's eyes lit up.

"No, Chuck. Donny's got to go back to bed," Jenny insisted.

"Aw, come on," Donny whined, grabbing for the mask.

"Aw, come on," Chuck repeated, sounding just like him. "It'll only take a second. And then Donny promises to go right back upstairs, don't you, pal?"

"Maybe," Donny said cautiously. He stood still while Chuck pulled the grotesque rubber mask down over his head. "How do I look?"

Both Jenny and Chuck burst out laughing. He looked so ridiculous, that gigantic head on such a skinny little body.

"Let me see! Let me see!" Donny yelled. He went running to the full-length mirror in the front hallway.

"Don't run!" Jenny called after him. Too late. Unable to see through the mask, he tripped over the sofa and fell hard against a mahogany end table. "Are you okay?" Jenny went running after him, giving Chuck a dirty look for causing all this trouble.

"I'm okay," Donny said, pulling himself up quickly and hurrying to the mirror.

"Kids are made of rubber," Chuck said to Jenny. "How do you look?" he called to Donny.

"Scary," Donny called back. "I'm a monster, and I'm going to eat you!" He came charging back into the living room, his arms outstretched.

"No! Don't eat me! Don't eat me!" Chuck ducked behind the couch. Then when Donny got near, he rolled over the couch, tumbled across the floor and hid behind one of the worn, over-stuffed armchairs.

"Grrrrrrr!" Donny roared, and charged again. He narrowly missed Chuck, who dodged away and ran toward the den, the monster in close pursuit.

"Chuck! Donny! Stop it! Donny has to go to bed!"

"He got me! He got me!" Chuck screamed as Donny leaped onto his back.

"Look, I'm not being paid to baby-sit two babies!" Jenny cried, exasperated.

"I'm not a baby!" Donny insisted, hurt.

Chuck pulled Donny off him and climbed slowly to his feet. "She's right," he told Donny softly. "It's past your bedtime. We'll play again next time. I'll bring the mask if you want."

"There won't be a next time," Jenny said flatly.

"Awww, you're mean," Donny told her.

"You heard him," Chuck agreed, laughing.

"Bring him next time," Donny told her.

"Yeah. Bring me next time."

"Chuck — stop it. Come on, Donny. I don't want to have to give your mom and dad a bad report. Back up to bed."

"Only if he tucks me in," Donny said, pointing at Chuck.

Jenny shrugged and rolled her eyes. "Do it," she told Chuck. "And no clowning around up there. Tuck him in and come right back."

"Aye, aye, Captain," Chuck said, saluting. He pulled off the mask and tossed it to the floor. Then taking Donny's hand, he led him up the stairs.

Jenny went to the den and, with a weary sigh, sank into the big, white leather armchair. She yawned. All of the tension must be making her tired, she thought.

Chuck certainly was great with Donny. The two of them just hit it off immediately. That's because Chuck's a big kid himself. Playing that stupid practical joke with the mask. Why did he do that? Did he really think I'd find it funny? Or was he trying to scare me to death?

"You look so cute when you're scared," he had said.

What a sick thing to say.

She heard Chuck's footsteps in the living room. "I'm in here, in the den," she called to him. He appeared in the doorway and slid beside her into the big armchair, putting his arm around her shoulder.

"Stop," she protested.

He snuggled against her. "I just want to apologize," he said softly in her ear. "That was stupid of me. I'm really sorry." He pressed his face against her cheek.

He kissed her. She turned her lips to his. She gave in to the kiss. Then, with a little cry, she pulled away.

She decided she had to ask. She had to ask about the phone calls. She had to know. She would never be able to trust him, never be comfortable with him, never be able to relax with him, to really believe in him, to really believe they could be a couple unless she knew.

She stood up and walked to the desk. He looked very hurt. "What's wrong?" he asked, that little-boy look again.

"I have to ask you something," she said, leaning back against the desk, looking away from him, looking at the bookshelves instead.

"What? Why do you look so grim? I said I was sorry about the mask."

"It's not the mask. I have to ask you about something else. I hope you'll understand. I just have to ask."

He shrugged. "Okay. I'll understand. Ask me anything." He forced a smile, but he looked very nervous.

"Someone has called me. Here at the Hagens." She turned and stared into his eyes. "Was it you?"

His face turned bright red. He opened his mouth but no sound came out. "Yes," he finally managed to whisper. "Yes. I'm sorry, Jenny. It was me."

Chapter 12

Her eyes burned into his.

He looked down at the dark floor. His face grew even redder. *He looks like a ripe tomato,* Jenny thought.

Her thoughts bounced around in her head as she tried to decide what to do now. He had admitted it. He had confessed. He was sick. He may be dangerous. She had to get him out of there, away from her, away from Donny.

She could still feel his mouth on hers, still taste him on her lips.

How could I have kissed him? How could I have actually liked someone who made those disgusting calls to me?

How awful. How tragic. How scary.

Chuck must be out of control. Sometimes he can hold himself in and be a funny, likable, good-natured guy. Other times, his other side comes out, his sick side, his evil side.

What should she do now?

"I — I was going to tell you," he said. His

voice cracked. He didn't say any more. He shook his head and stared at the floor. "I — I didn't mean — "

A loud crash interrupted him. "Where'd that come from?" he asked quickly, looking up, obviously glad for the interruption.

"Not upstairs," Jenny said, heading to the doorway. It was more of a prayer than a statement.

He jumped to his feet and followed her across the living room. "No. It was outside. In the back, I think."

"I'm going to check upstairs," Jenny said, taking the stairs two at a time. Donny was sleeping peacefully, a stuffed tiger held tightly to his chest. They look just like Calvin and Hobbes, she thought. She hurried through the other upstairs rooms, not bothering to turn on the lights, hoping against hope that she wouldn't see or hear anything — or anyone.

She didn't.

Chuck was right. The crash must have been outside. She hurried downstairs and called to him. He was in the kitchen, looking out the window in the kitchen door. "See anything?" she asked.

"No. Not a thing. Guess we should forget about it."

"No. It was a loud crash. I can't ignore it. I'm in charge here. It had to be caused by something. By someone. By I-don't-know-what."

"Calm down, Jenny." He started to put his hands on her shoulders to comfort her, but she backed away. He immediately remembered why, and his face filled with embarrassment and shame.

"Okay. Let's call the police," he suggested, heading to the wall phone.

"No. Wait." She pulled his hand off the receiver. "What if it's nothing? A raccoon in the garbage or something? I don't want the police out. I don't want the Hagens to think I get hysterical and can't handle stupid little things."

He shrugged. "Okay. Then we'll ignore it."

She didn't reply. Instead she walked over to the sink and began searching frantically through the cabinet drawers. Finally she found what she was looking for, a silver-and-black flashlight. She tested it. "Good and bright," she said, shining it in Chuck's face.

He threw up his hands to shield his eyes. "What are you doing?"

"Going out to investigate," she said, pulling open the kitchen door. "You watch from here. If you see or hear anything wrong, call the police."

"But, Jenny — "

She was already out the door, following the narrow beam of light from the flashlight toward the garage.

The air smelled clean and fresh. She took a deep breath. Someone in a house nearby had a fire going. The dry fragrance of burning cedar invaded her nose, made the air smell warm and sweet. She turned back. Chuck was watching her from the kitchen.

Am I safer out here than inside with him? she

asked herself sadly. What do I think I'm going to find out here? I already know that the creep who made those horrible, threatening calls is already in the house, watching me from the kitchen.

Jenny shivered. Twigs cracked loudly under her feet. The ground felt as hard as rock. She shined the light around the yard, bouncing it along the tall, wooden fence at the back. Nothing there.

Round piles of leaves looked like craters in the dark. There was no wind now. The trees were still, silent onlookers.

What was *that* moving to her left?

Just a tall shrub. She took a deep breath and let it out slowly. The evergreen shrub was the same height as a person. But it stood straight and unmoving. Her imagination was playing tricks on her again.

She shined the white light onto other shrubs that dotted the yard. No sign of anything wrong. No sign of anything. Or anyone.

The crash had been loud, and it had been nearby.

"Maybe it *was* just a raccoon in a trash can," she told herself. But where was the trash can?

She followed a flagstone walk down a slightly sloping incline toward the garage.

Hold on a minute!

The garage light. Hadn't there been a bright yellow spotlight on the side of the garage when she arrived? It was dark now. No light at all.

Maybe she remembered incorrectly. Maybe the spotlight hadn't been on. But if it hadn't, how did she remember one being there?

She felt a sudden chill. It was cold out, cold enough to see her breath, hot and wet in front of her face, misting in the wavering light of the flashlight. She should have put on her jacket.

Maybe the spotlight had burned out. That was possible.

She heard a scraping sound. Shoes scraping against the hard ground? She raised the flashlight to the side of the garage.

She heard the scraping again.

Someone coughed. A man.

The scraping sound again, coming from the garage.

Jenny clicked off the flashlight.

Now what?

Call out to him? Try to sneak up on him? Run back to the house?

She clicked the flashlight back on, illuminating the garage door. The door was open. She could see snow tires hanging on the wall. A few lawn chairs. A small two-wheeler that must be Donny's.

She heard more scraping, boots against concrete, the concrete garage floor.

The man coughed again.

"Who's there?"

She didn't recognize her own voice. She hadn't meant to call out. Her heart was pounding now. She struggled to keep the light steady.

"Who's there?" she repeated, louder.

A man stepped into the circle of light.

"Sorry. Hope I didn't frighten you." He smiled at her.

It was Willers, the next-door neighbor. He was wearing the same plaid lumberjack shirt. He took a few steps toward her, then stopped. "I'm really sorry. You look frightened. Please don't be. It's only me." His voice was as rough as sandpaper. The way he kept insisting that Jenny shouldn't be frightened scared her even more.

"What are you doing back here, Mr. Willers?" she managed to say.

"I thought I saw a prowler. Back here in the Hagens' yard. I wanted to make sure that — "

The prowler story again. Willers didn't make it sound too believable.

"But what was that crash?" Jenny interrupted impatiently, keeping the light on Willers' dark, stubbled face.

"Crash? Oh. I tripped over Hagen's firewood pile. Sent the logs crashing." He pointed to the logs by the garage wall. They were scattered in disarray. "I'll pick them up for him in the morning."

"But — you have no flashlight. You came out without a light? Without anything?"

Willers smiled, a crooked smile, a smile that seemed to admit he had been caught lying. "I wanted to sneak up on the guy," he said. "You know, take him by surprise."

Suddenly the smile faded. "Are you all alone

in there?" he asked, his dark eyes searching for something in hers.

The question caught Jenny off guard. The way he said it, the rumble of his rough voice, sounded just like the whisperer on the phone.

But Chuck had already confessed. Chuck was the whisperer on the phone.

"No," Jenny told him. "I'm not alone. A friend is over. A friend came over to keep me company."

"I see," Willers said, scratching his black stubbly beard. "I wondered about the car parked out front."

What a snoop, Jenny thought. Does he spend all of his time watching the Hagens' house?

They stood staring at each other for a while. Jenny couldn't think of anything else to say. She shivered, almost dropping the flashlight.

"You'd better get inside," Willers said. "You'll catch your death."

Why did he say it that way? Was that some kind of threat?

"There's no prowler out here," he said. "Maybe I scared him away. Go on. Go back in. Sorry I scared you."

"Okay," Jenny said. "Night." She watched him walk away until he disappeared into the trees at the right of the yard.

By the time she got back to the kitchen, she was trembling all over. "You poor thing," Chuck said, taking her hands in his and rubbing them to warm them. "You were so brave. Come here. Let me warm you up."

She pulled away from him again. "No, Chuck. Let go."

"Jenny, that man out there — "

"Just the neighbor. He accidentally knocked over the woodpile. That was the crash. Now I think you'd better go."

"But, I want to — "

"No. I think you should just go. I don't think we have anything to talk about."

"Yes, we do," he said, suddenly sounding more forceful, as if he had just made up his mind about something. He pulled out a tall kitchen stool and climbed onto it. "I'm not leaving until you listen to me."

"I told you, Chuck. There's nothing more to say."

"But I want to explain, Jenny. About calling you. I know it wasn't right. I mean, I know there's no excuse for it. But I want to explain. Then I'll go. I promise."

She leaned back against the counter and closed her eyes. "Okay. Explain."

"Saturday night I got the Hagens' phone number from your mother."

"I know."

"I was just going to call and say hi. You know, just talk, nothing important. I thought maybe you were bored here all by yourself and we could talk. We could get to know each other better."

"Chuck, really — "

"Jenny, please — don't interrupt. This is really hard for me."

It's true, he really did look as if he were suffering. He had his hands so tightly clamped onto the back of the stool that his knuckles were white. His eyes kept darting back and forth. His chin was trembling as he talked.

"Sorry. Go on," Jenny said.

"Okay. I was really nervous about calling you. I mean, I'd never called you before. And you probably won't believe this, but I'm really very shy. I mean, all my joking and clowning around, I guess that's kind of a cover-up. I just do that because I'm nervous a lot of the time around people. I get scared, scared that they'll think I'm weird, or they won't like me, or something."

He was fidgeting on the kitchen stool. He wiped his sweaty hands off on his jeans legs. "So it isn't easy for me to call a girl, especially a girl I like a lot, like you. But I called you anyway. It took me over an hour to work up the courage to call — do you believe that?"

"I'm sorry," Jenny said.

"And when you picked up the phone, I guess I just panicked. I completely forgot what I was going to say. I started breathing real heavy. I felt weird, paralyzed, almost like I was going to faint or something. I wanted to talk to you, but I couldn't make a sound.

"It was so stupid. I heard you saying, 'Hello, hello,' and I was just too panicked to talk. So I hung up. After I calmed down, I felt ridiculous. And I realized you probably thought it was some kind of a nut or a joker calling."

111

"All I could hear was breathing," Jenny said. "I thought it was a creep who calls girls up and breathes at them."

"I'm really sorry. I was going to tell you on Sunday at the mall what had happened, but it was too embarrassing. I just wanted to forget about it. I had such a good time with you, I didn't want to spoil it by telling you what a dopey nerd I am in real life."

He wiped his hands again on his jeans legs. He was staring down at the linoleum floor, but he looked really relieved, as if he had gotten a great weight off his chest.

"Go on," Jenny said.

He looked up, confused. "What?"

"Go on. Tell me about the rest of the calls."

"What? What calls? That was it."

"What do you mean, Chuck? I want to hear your explanation for the rest."

"Jenny, there is no rest. I only made one call. It was such a disaster, do you think I'd call back?"

"But I got other calls. Someone whispering threats. Threatening to come here. Asking if I was all alone."

"Huh?"

"Saturday night. And tonight."

"Jenny, that's horrible! And you thought I made them?"

"No. I mean — I didn't know. When you said you were the one, I — "

"I only called once. You've got to believe me." He looked at her. "You *do* believe me — don't you?"

She ran to him in reply. She was in his arms. She was returning his kiss. He felt so warm, so good, so safe.

Did she believe him?

She wanted to. She really wanted to. . . .

But she wasn't sure.

Chapter 13

Twenty minutes later, they were still kissing on the white leather chair in the den when they heard a car door slam.

"The Hagens! They must be home early!" Jenny cried, shoving Chuck off the chair. He looked confused for a second, then realized why Jenny was so panicky.

"I'm out of here!" he cried. "Which way?"

"Go out the back! No — the front! Quick! The front! Get out of here!" Jenny screamed. Was that the back door opening? If so, the Hagens would be in the hallway in seconds. Could Chuck get out in time?

He flew across the living room, pulled open the front door, and vanished without looking back. "The door! You left the door open!" Jenny called, even though he was already out, already running through the darkness of the leaf-cluttered lawn toward his car.

Jenny slammed the front door just as she heard the kitchen door open. She glanced anxiously at the living room, trying to make sure no trace of Chuck had been left behind.

A few seconds later, Mr. Hagen came hurrying into the room, followed closely by Mrs. Hagen, who looked very upset and annoyed.

"You've got to stop doing this, Mike," she said, the tension in her voice revealing that this argument had been steaming for some time. "We had no reason to leave the Fischers' so early. Jenny is perfectly capable of — "

"Is Donny okay?" Mr. Hagen asked Jenny, ignoring his wife. His cheeks and ears were aflame. His small, steel-colored eyes burned into Jenny's, as if searching for trouble she might be trying to conceal.

"Fine," Jenny said, her heart still pounding over Chuck's narrow escape. "Just fine."

Mr. Hagen spun around, grabbed the bannister in his big hand, and bounded up the stairs, taking them two at a time despite his limp. Mrs. Hagen shrugged and rolled her eyes. She suddenly looked very tired and old.

Jenny didn't know what to say to her. She felt very awkward. And she felt bad that Mr. Hagen still didn't trust her.

But then, why should he trust me? she asked herself. I've been in the den making out with Chuck all this time instead of staying alert and doing my job.

"Donny was good tonight," she told Mrs. Hagen, trying to sound calm and normal, as if she didn't notice the Hagens were having a fight.

"He's a good boy," Mrs. Hagen said, wearily

pulling off her coat and draping it over the bannister.

Mr. Hagen reappeared at the top of the stairs, still looking troubled. "Donny's fine," he told his wife.

"Of course, he is," Mrs. Hagen said, frowning. "I'm sick of you and your hunches and bad premonitions, Mike. Donny's in good hands here. You have no cause for such alarm."

Again he ignored her and turned to Jenny. "I thought I saw a car out front, parked across the street," he said, leaning heavily on the bannister as he descended. "Do you know anything about it?"

"No. No, I don't," Jenny lied.

He limped over to the living room window, pushed aside the heavy drapes, and peered out. "That's funny." His voice was muffled by the drapes, making him sound far away. "I could have sworn it was parked right across the street. Not there now. . . ."

He stood looking out for a long while. When he returned, he looked at Jenny suspiciously. She wondered if he could read the guilt on her face. "You didn't hear any car doors or anything?"

"No. Not a sound. I was in the den most of the time." She wasn't a very good liar. Was he staring at her like that because he knew she was lying?

"You forgot to get Jenny's coat when you were upstairs," Mrs. Hagen said, obvious about trying to change the subject.

"That's okay. I'll go get it," Jenny said, eager to get going.

"No. No. I'll go," Mr. Hagen insisted. He was already halfway up the stairs.

"He had a bad day," Mrs. Hagen confided to Jenny as soon as he was out of earshot. "He's been under a lot of pressure, as I told you. Did everything go okay?"

"Well . . . actually," Jenny started reluctantly, "something kind of strange happened. This neighbor of yours — "

"Sshhh — he's coming back," Mrs. Hagen whispered. "Please — don't trouble him with it tonight." She gave Jenny a pleading look.

He handed Jenny her coat and headed back into the living room. "I'm going up to bed," Mrs. Hagen said, yawning. She patted Jenny on the shoulder and smiled. "G'night. See you Saturday."

"Wait a minute! What's this?" Mr. Hagen cried from the living room, sounding alarmed.

Oh no, Jenny thought. Did Chuck leave his jacket? No. He wasn't wearing a jacket. What could it be?

She hurried into the living room. Mr. Hagen was holding the rubber monster mask up by the long, red plastic hair, its protruding eyeballs flopping around in front of him. Chuck must have left it on the couch.

Mr. Hagen looked at her suspiciously. "Where'd this come from?"

"Oh. That silly mask," Jenny said, thinking

fast, forcing a smile to her face. "I brought it for Donny. I thought maybe he'd think it was funny."

The suspicious look didn't leave Mr. Hagen's face. He held the mask up and examined it closely. "Funny. I didn't see it when you came in."

"I had it in my backpack," Jenny said. "I'll take it home." She took it out of Mr. Hagen's hands. "Donny didn't really like it."

"He wasn't scared of it, was he?" he asked, a thin smile breaking over his face.

"No. I don't think so. He just said it was gross," Jenny told him. She hurried to get her backpack and stuff the mask inside. She didn't want it lying around the next morning. Maybe if he didn't see it, Donny wouldn't mention to his parents that a boy named Chuck had brought it.

"Mike, why are you cross-examining Jenny like that?" Mrs. Hagen asked from the doorway.

He looked up, surprised that she was still downstairs. "Was I? Gee, I'm sorry, Jenny. I didn't mean to. I guess I'm a little wound up tonight."

"That's okay," Jenny said brightly. "I'm ready to go now."

Driving her home, Mr. Hagen did seem more troubled than usual. He talked nonstop, his thoughts rambling from one subject to another, first talking about Donny and his schoolwork, then about a tree house he planned to build for Donny, then about a dog he'd had when he was Donny's age and how it had disappeared.

When they stopped for a stoplight a few blocks from her home, he finally grew silent. He turned to her with a serious look on his face. "There's probably no need to tell you this," he said softly, "but I like to make things clear. I have one important rule for our baby-sitters. And that's no visitors. I know a lot of times baby-sitters like to invite their friends over to keep them company. I guess some parents allow it, or at least, put up with it. But I don't. I just don't think it's a good idea. I want all of your attention on Donny. I hope you understand."

The light had changed, but he didn't move. Why was he saying this now? Did he figure out about Chuck's car parked across the street? About the mask? Could he read her mind?

"Yes. Sure, I do," Jenny said. "I understand." She could feel her face getting hot from the guilt she felt. She was glad he couldn't see her blushing in the darkness.

He pressed on the gas and the car rolled forward. "We had another child," he said, staring straight ahead through the windshield, his face suddenly blank, completely expressionless.

Jenny shifted in the seat and stared at him, waiting for him to say more. But he didn't. The words hung in the air. He seemed lost in thought. He stared straight ahead in silence the rest of the way to Jenny's house.

"Good night, Mr. Hagen," she said, climbing out of the car.

He didn't seem to hear her.

She slammed the door and watched him drive away, still staring straight ahead.

"Rotate! ROTATE!"

Miss Marks's powerful voice echoed off the tile of the gym walls. "Rotate, girls! Your serve, Jenny!"

"God, I hate volleyball," Jenny muttered to Laura as she switched to serve position on the floor, the other girls on her team all moving over one place.

"Here's a tip that might help you," Laura told her, leaning forward to catch her breath, her hands resting above her knees.

"What's that?" Jenny asked.

"Try to get it over the net this time!"

A few girls laughed. Jenny scowled at her friend, brought back her arm, raised the ball, and punched it with all her might.

Once again, it sailed into the net.

"One more try," Miss Marks called, looking on disapprovingly from the side of the net. "Get under it, Jenny. Get under it."

"I wish *you'd* get under it," Jenny muttered under her breath.

"What?" Miss Marks called.

"I said I'll try," Jenny told her. She raised the ball and brought her fist up fast and hard. This time the ball sailed under the net.

"Serve goes to the Blues. Rotate. ROTATE!" Miss Marks shouted.

Jenny kicked at the floor, feeling like a fool

and a failure. She looked up and caught Laura laughing at her.

"Well, you're certainly hostile today," she said. "What's your problem?"

The ball came flying over the net. Jenny tipped it straight up in the air. Sarah Robbins leaped and batted it over to the other side.

"Oh, I don't know," Laura said, slapping the ball easily over the net. "I guess I'm in a bad mood because I broke up with Bob Tanner last night."

"WHAT??"

"Rotate! ROTATE!"

"Laura, are you serious? Ulllp!"

The ball bounced off Jenny's chest. Her breath shot out like a balloon popping. She uttered a strangled protest and dropped to the gym floor. The lights seemed to flicker and flash. She tried to get up, but she was too dizzy.

Miss Marks's whistle blew. "TIME!" Jenny looked up to see the copper-haired gym instructor leaning over her. "You're okay, Jenny. You just had the wind knocked out."

If I had the wind knocked out, how can I be okay? Jenny thought. But she didn't say anything. She wasn't sure she could talk. She was still struggling to breathe normally.

"Laura, take Jenny to the locker room," Miss Marks instructed, patting Jenny on the back of her T-shirt, then jumping back up and returning to the game.

"ROTATE! ROTATE!"

Miss Marks's voice reverberated over the ringing in Jenny's ears as Laura led her slowly away. "It's okay. I can walk," Jenny said, pulling away from Laura.

"Listen, Jen. I'm sorry. That was my fault," Laura said, sweeping her hair off her shoulder. "Whew. Is it hot in here, or what?"

"It was my fault," Jenny said, her voice still thin and shaky. "I should've been watching."

"Can you breathe?"

"Yeah. I'm fine. Really," Jenny said, dropping down onto the wooden bench in front of her gym locker. "I feel a little light, that's all. You know, kind of feathery. But I'll be okay."

"Want me to sit with you for a while?"

"No. Really, Laura. You can go back to the game. I'm just going to catch my breath. Then I'll take a shower."

"Okay. See you later, Jen."

"Hey, Laura — sorry about you and Bob."

"Way it goes," Laura said, shrugging her tiny shoulders, and vanishing out the locker room door.

Jenny felt very dizzy. She leaned forward, elbows on her thighs, resting her head in her hands. After a while, the dizziness passed. Her head felt better, but her stomach felt as if it had a huge rock inside it. She opened her locker door and reached for her bag to get a tissue.

Inside the bag, her hand came upon a folded-up sheet of yellow notebook paper. She pulled it out. She didn't remember putting it in there.

She unfolded the sheet of paper. It appeared

to be some kind of a note. As she read it, she began to get dizzy again:

HI, BABES.

ALL ALONE IN THAT BIG OLD HOUSE?
DON'T WORRY. COMPANY'S COMING.

The bag fell out of her lap, spilling her hairbrush and mirror and several other items onto the concrete floor. She didn't notice. Her head was spinning. Her stomach ached.

She read the note again.

Again.

The big, block letters, printed so neatly, so carefully, seemed to jump off the yellow page at her.

COMPANY'S COMING.
DON'T WORRY. COMPANY'S COMING.

Who wrote it? Who folded it up and shoved it into her bag?

The phone caller and the note writer had to be the same person. But who? Who could have gotten to her bag?

Her heart skipped a beat as she mouthed the name of the only person who had been close enough to her bag last night to slip the note in.

Chuck. . . .

Chapter 14

The bus lurched and bumped across town. Since Jenny and a man in overalls, stretched out sound asleep on the long backseat, were the only passengers on this blustery Saturday evening, the bus driver was setting a crosstown record. He wasn't stopping at bus stops or even for traffic lights!

The town seemed really empty, as if the cold and the gloom had forced everyone into hibernation even though the winter was just beginning. Staring out of the smeared bus window at the silent streets and empty sidewalks, Jenny felt as dark and gloomy as the passing scenery.

Her stop came much too quickly. For a brief moment, she was tempted to stay on the bus, to keep riding round and round from one side of town to the other until the night was over. Only the thought of seeing Donny cheered her, made her forget her trepidation at going back to the Hagens' house, where so much fear awaited.

She stepped down off the bus, ducking her head to protect her eyes from the wind, which seemed to gust in all directions at once. The bare trees tossed and rattled their branches as she zipped up her down jacket as far as it would go and began to hurry toward the Hagens' house.

Friday's rainfall had frozen, leaving icy patches scattered over the lawns and sidewalk. Jenny slipped and almost toppled over backwards, but her speed propelled her forward and she regained her balance without slowing down.

She had gone nearly a block when she began to suspect she was being followed.

Walking even faster, she tried to listen over the roar of the wind. Was it just the clatter of tree branches overhead? Was she imagining it?

No. She heard ice cracking beneath someone's boots. Footsteps moving quickly over the frozen walk. Heavy breathing.

She turned her head quickly, saw moving shadows. Shadows sliding closer, closer. . . .

It was Willers, the creepy neighbor.

She began to run, slipping again, sucking in the frozen, wet air, running past dark, shifting woods now, no houses in sight, the entire world lit by a lone street lamp, casting more shadow than light, shadows that swirled and teased and tried to bewilder her as she fled.

Run, Jenny.

Run.

She wasn't fast enough.

She couldn't outrun him.

She *had* to outrun him.

"Wait up!" he called. But she just kept running.

A few seconds later, she was leaping onto the Hagens' front stoop, grateful for the yellow porch light, so bright, so warming, so safe. She looked back to see if Willers was behind her, but he had disappeared into the darkness.

Where had he gone? Why was he chasing her? Was he trying to terrorize her?

She realized she was shivering from the cold.

She raised her hand to knock — and the door swung open.

"Jenny, I *thought* I heard someone out here." Mr. Hagen said.

She dashed into the narrow front hallway, so grateful to be inside.

"Jenny — what's wrong?" he asked. "You look terrible."

"I'm sorry. Someone followed me from the bus stop."

"What? What are you talking about? Who?" He helped her pull off her down jacket.

"Mr. Willers. Your neighbor."

"Willers? I don't know anyone named Willers."

"He said he was your next-door neighbor."

Mr. Hagen held the jacket in front of him and stared at her, looking really troubled. "Neighbor? What neighbor? Jenny, we have no neighbors. That house next door has been vacant for six months!"

Chapter 15

"Can we play hide-and-seek?"

"Not now, Donny," Jenny said, giving his slender shoulders a gentle squeeze.

"This man said he was a neighbor? Said his name was Willers?" Mr. Hagen asked, his face aflame. He stood blocking the entrance to the living room, Jenny's jacket in his hand.

"I'm pretty sure I heard correctly," Jenny said.

"Maybe we shouldn't go out tonight," Mr. Hagen called upstairs to his wife.

She appeared at the top of the stairs, snapping on her earrings, a surprised look on her face. "What? Mike, you know the Spaldings are counting on us. Elaine will never speak to me again if we don't show up."

"But what about the attacks on those babysitters?" Mr. Hagen called, his face consumed with worry. "Donny could be in danger. Maybe this Willers — "

"Mike, we *have* to go," Mrs. Hagen called

down. "I'm sure if Jenny keeps the doors locked and all the lights on — "

"Okay, okay," he replied impatiently. "We won't stay out too late," he told Jenny. "If you hear anything at all, the tiniest squeak or creak, call the police. They can be here in less than five minutes."

"Okay," Jenny said. She had every intention of calling the police at the first suspicious sign. She reached into her jeans pocket and felt the piece of paper on which she had written Lieutenant Ferris's special number.

"What about hide-and-seek?" Donny whined, pulling Jenny toward the living room. "You promised!"

"I did not!" Jenny said, laughing. "I did not promise."

"No hide-and-seek tonight," Mr. Hagen said sternly. "Do something quieter. Why don't you watch that tape you made me rent for you?"

"Yeah! Yeah!" Donny cried enthusiastically, tugging Jenny harder. "Come on. Let's watch it."

"What is it?" Jenny asked, relieved that she wouldn't have to go running all over the house tonight playing hide-and-seek. "What did you rent?"

"*Poltergeist*," Donny said. "Have you seen it? It's really cool. She gets sucked into the TV set and she can't get out."

"Oh, great," Jenny said, rolling her eyes. Just what I needed tonight, she thought.

Donny settled down on the floor in front of the TV, and Jenny started the movie for him. The

Hagens left, after three more warnings by Mr. Hagen to call the police if she heard anything at all. He looked so overcome with worry, she was a little sorry she had told him about Willers. "Poor Mr. Hagen," Jenny told herself as the movie rolled across the TV screen. "*I'm* the one who should be scared. But he looked positively terrified!"

The movie seemed to be a series of loud, disconnected scenes. She couldn't concentrate on it at all. Donny kept insisting that he'd rather play hide-and-seek, and she kept refusing. Luckily he was falling asleep before the movie was half over. She got him up to bed before nine-thirty.

Now what? she asked herself, returning to the white leather chair in the den. I've got to do something to get my mind off Willers, and Chuck, and the calls, and the folded-up note, and . . . Chuck.

Was it just two nights ago that they had sat in this chair together . . . so together. . . .

She stared at the black telephone across the den on the desk. Was it going to ring tonight? Was her whispering caller going to renew his threats? Or did he plan to carry them out tonight?

She shuddered.

Then she heard the footsteps.

Someone was running fast in the back hallway. Donny?

No. The footsteps were too heavy, too fast.

Who was in the house?

She jumped up, reached in her pocket for the phone number. Would she have time to call?

No.

The footsteps were closer. Someone was running across the living room.

"MR. HAGEN!"

"Hi, Jenny." He limped toward her at full speed. His face red, filled with worry. "Everything okay?"

"Yes. You startled me. I didn't know who — "

"I hurried back. I just had a hunch. A hunch that something was wrong." He was breathing heavily, wheezing between his words. His shirt had come untucked from his trousers. He looked positively crazed with fear.

"Donny's fine. He went to bed early." Jenny squeaked out the words. She was still trying to calm down after the fright he had given her.

"He's okay? You're sure? He isn't sick or anything?"

"No. He's fine. Really."

"I just had a hunch. A bad feeling that something was terribly wrong."

She watched him clamber up the stairs until he disappeared on the landing. Then she slumped down on the bottom step, rested her head in her hands, trying to collect herself.

How many more times was Mr. Hagen going to frighten her like that? Would he ever trust her? Would he ever learn to relax? He had been so overcome with fear for Donny he hadn't even apologized for scaring her to death!

And what did he expect to find? What was he so afraid of?

Jenny pulled herself to her feet and leaned all

her weight against the bannister, waiting for Mr. Hagen to return from Donny's room. She yawned. Fear always seemed to make her feel tired.

"JENNY! JENNY!" Mr. Hagen's cries shattered her thoughts, startled her awake.

"Yes?"

He glared down at her from the top of the stairs. His normally small eyes were wide with terror. His face was twisted in shock.

"Donny's gone!" he screamed. "GONE!"

Chapter 16

"Where is he? Where IS he?" Mr. Hagen was screaming from the top of the stairs.

His words had no meaning for Jenny. Her mind had gone blank. She could hear his shouts, hear the sounds he was making, but the sounds had no meaning, as if the words were too horrifying to comprehend.

"This can't be happening to me," she told herself.

"Donny! Where are you?" Mr. Hagen shouted at the top of his lungs. "Where is he? WHERE IS HE??"

Jenny saw flashes of light, like flashcubes being popped right in front of her face. She blinked, trying to get away from the flashes, trying to see clearly.

"Donny! Donny! Where are you?" Mr. Hagen's voice was calling.

More flashing lights. Jenny struggled to clear her head, to force herself back to reality, to force the words to make sense again, to make this all go away.

Without realizing it, she had climbed the stairs. She was running into Donny's room.

If only the white flashes would stop.

If only she would wake up to find this was just a nightmare.

If only Mr. Hagen would stop shouting, maybe she could clear her head, figure it out, take responsibility.

"This can't be happening!" Mr. Hagen screamed at her. "Not again!"

What?

What did he say?

She stared at him, stared into his frightened eyes, stared into his red face, swollen in horror and panic, trying to see into his mind, trying to make sense of what he said.

"Where is he? Where is Donny?" He paced the small bedroom frantically, his limp more pronounced, his face so scarlet Jenny thought he might explode, repeating his question again and again, no longer able to shout, his voice a dry whisper.

"Donny — where are you?"

"Here I am," Donny said brightly, crawling out from under his bed.

He climbed to his feet and straightened his pajamas. "Gotcha!" he told Jenny, and started to laugh, pounding his little fists gleefully on top of his rumpled bedspread.

Jenny and Mr. Hagen were so startled, so overwhelmed by the sight of Donny, in perfect shape, unharmed, laughing, enjoying his ghastly joke, they stood staring at him openmouthed, almost afraid to move, afraid that if they made a sound or came closer, he'd disappear again.

And then Mr. Hagen let out a roar, a wild animal's roar, a roar of unleashed emotion. He lunged at Donny, picked him up by the waist, and pulled him close to his chest. "You're okay. You're okay. You're okay!" he cried again and again, hugging the surprised boy tightly to his chest.

"I was playing hide-and-seek," Donny offered, suddenly seeing the need to explain. "Jenny wouldn't play, so I played by myself."

"What on earth is going on up here? What's all the shouting about?" Mrs. Hagen burst into the room, her coat swirling behind her. She stared at her red-faced husband, squeezing Donny so tightly, still repeating, "You're okay, you're okay" into the boy's ear.

"Why are you doing that to Donny, Mike? You're squeezing him too hard!"

"We had a little scare," Jenny told her, finally finding her voice again, the flashing lights beginning to fade, her pulse beginning to return to normal.

"A scare? What kind of a scare?" she asked Jenny, walking across the room and pulling Donny away from Mr. Hagen.

"I was playing hide-and-seek," Donny reported with more than a little pride. "I fooled them. I fooled them both."

"Get back in bed, Donny," Mrs. Hagen said

sternly. "It's way past your bedtime." She turned angrily to her husband. "What are you doing here? Why did you leave the party? I thought you were downstairs shooting pool with Jack and Ernie. I didn't even know you had left."

"I just ran out for a minute. I had a hunch, a hunch something was wrong with Donny. I had to run home to find out. Then — "

"Look at you," Mrs. Hagen said, her anger softening as she realized how overwrought her husband was. "You're a wreck. You've got to stop this needless worrying, Mike. I mean it. You had no business running home like this. I'm very worried about you. Very worried."

Mr. Hagen looked past her to Jenny. "Please — let's not have a fight in front of — "

"I — I'll go downstairs," Jenny said uncertainly. "Now that we know Donny is okay, I — "

"No. Let's get your coat while we're upstairs," Mr. Hagen said. "I'll drive you home."

"No, you won't," Mrs. Hagen said, taking his arm. "I'm going to give you some pills to calm you down, Mike. I want you to stay home and try to get yourself together. I'll drive Jenny home."

"I'm together. Really," he insisted.

"Can I go, too?" Donny interrupted.

"No. Of course not," Mrs. Hagen said sternly. "You'd better be asleep in five minutes, Donny, or you're going to be in a lot of trouble." She shooed Jenny and Mr. Hagen from the room. "Go on. Out of here!"

Mr. Hagen retrieved Jenny's coat from his bedroom closet. Then, over his wife's objections, he grabbed the car keys and ushered Jenny out the door.

They rode in silence the entire way.

Normally Jenny would have found that very uncomfortable. Tonight she was grateful.

When he pulled up her driveway, he turned to her with a guilty half-smile. "I really should apologize," he said.

"No. It isn't necessary."

"I really should," he said. But then he stopped. His eyes were wet. Was he crying?

"I really should," he repeated. His voice sounded choked and small.

"Donny put us both through a real scare," Jenny said, and slid out of the car. She leaned back into the car, expecting Mr. Hagen to say something else. But he didn't, so she closed the door and hurried inside.

"You're home early," her mother said. She was in her bathrobe, bare feet up on the couch, reading one of her mystery novels.

"I know. The Hagens came home early," Jenny said. "Just as well." She yawned. "I'm really tired. Good night." No point in worrying her mother with all that was going on.

"Night," her mother replied, not looking up from the book.

Jenny climbed the narrow stairs to her room. Wish I could have a quiet Saturday night, she thought. Sitting home, reading a good book sounded pretty good.

She tossed her jacket onto her desk chair. Just a few more weeks. I'm going to work a few more weeks. Then I'll have more than enough money for Christmas. I'll tell the Hagens I have to quit, that it's interfering with my schoolwork. Maybe I'll baby-sit occasionally for Donny. But no more of this twice a week grind. No more frightening neighbors. No more frightening notes or creepy phone calls.

Just as she thought this, the phone on her desk rang.

She jumped and let out a startled cry.

Who would be calling this late on a Saturday night?

Laura? No. Laura would be out on a date with whoever had replaced Bob Tanner.

A second ring.

Was the creep following her? Did he have her home phone number?

A third ring.

"Jenny, aren't you going to answer that?" her mother called from downstairs.

She picked up the receiver. "Hello?"

"Hi."

"Chuck?"

"Yeah."

For a second, she was relieved. But her suspicions about Chuck quickly brought back her feeling of dread.

"Oh. Hi. I'm surprised. I mean — "

"I wanted to talk to you."

"Oh?"

"Jenny, you've been avoiding me."

"No, I — "

"Yes, you have. Come on. You walked away from me twice in the hall at school yesterday. And once I saw you deliberately go the other way when you saw me coming."

"I've just been busy, Chuck, and really — "

"Is it about Thursday night? Did I get you into trouble? Did Hagen see my car? I'm really sorry, Jenny."

"No. He saw the car, but he didn't know anything."

"Then what's the problem? I kind of got the idea that you liked me. And I like you. A lot. You know this is hard for me to do, call like this. So I wish you'd be honest with me. It's about that call I made, isn't it? When I scared you. I told you how sorry I was. I'll apologize a thousand times, if you want."

He sounded so sweet. And so sincere. He wasn't joking or trying to be funny. He really cared about her, Jenny thought. Once again, she began to feel guilty for suspecting him.

"I haven't been avoiding you. I've just had a lot on my mind. I got a scary note, Chuck. I found it in my bag. Someone had to be pretty close to me to put it there."

"And you thought it was me?" He sounded really hurt.

"I didn't know what to think. I still don't. I'm very mixed up."

"Why don't I come over and we'll talk?"

"No. It's too late. I'm exhausted. Donny

played a mean joke tonight and had us all in a panic."

"How about Thursday night?" he asked eagerly. Too eagerly? "We could study together. Please. I'll leave really early."

"Well. . . ." She didn't know what to say. She wanted to trust him. She wanted to be with him. But she just couldn't get rid of her suspicions. "Okay. I'll call Laura. Maybe she'd like to come, too. We can all study together." Safety in numbers, she thought.

"Well, okay. I guess." He sounded very disappointed. He laughed to cover it up. "You really think we need a chaperone?"

She forced a laugh, too. "Laura's my best friend. I like to spend time with her, too, you know."

"Okay. Good. Well, I'd better get off. Good night, Jenny."

"Night, Chuck."

"Thursday night will be special," he said. Then he hung up.

What did he mean by that?

Did his voice sound really strange when he said that?

Or was Jenny just imagining it?

Chapter 17

"Wipe that fiendish look off your face — this instant!" Jenny scolded.

Donny moved his hand down over his face as if using it to wipe off his expression. In its place, was a dopey, twisted grin.

"Wipe that expression off, too," Jenny said, unable to keep a straight face. "No hide-and-seek tonight. No more tricks on your baby-sitter. Understand?"

"Maybe," he said slyly, climbing into bed.

She ran her hand through his soft hair and pulled up his covers. "Now, go right to sleep."

"Is that boy coming over?" he asked, yawning.

"That's none of your business," Jenny said lightly. She felt a sudden pang of guilt. Had Donny told his parents about Chuck's visit?

I don't care, she thought as she descended the stairs. I don't want to be alone here. I'm glad Chuck and Laura are coming.

A few minutes later, she heard a knock on the door. She started to pull it open, thought better of it, and cautiously called out, "Who's there?"

"The Three Stooges," Chuck replied through the door.

Three?

She gratefully pulled open the door to find Chuck, Laura, and Eugene. "Hi, Eugene," she cried, unable to hide her surprise.

"How's it goin'?" he said, following the others into the entranceway. "Wow. Some house!"

"Looks more like a museum than a house," Laura said, pulling off her coat and tossing it onto the stairs.

Jenny gave Laura a look, as if to say, "What's Eugene doing here?" Laura just shrugged. "Why not?" she mouthed.

"Is this place a horror show, or what?" Chuck laughed, picking up a strange sculpture of an unrecognizable animal and examining it. "It's so creepy-looking. Can't you just picture vampires sleeping in coffins in the basement?"

Jenny gave Chuck a dirty look. "Stop that. Is that how you cheer me up?"

"Oops — sorry." He pretended to stab himself in the chest and then fell backwards onto the sofa in front of the fireplace.

"Hey, didn't anyone bring any books? I thought we were going to study," Jenny said.

"I knew we forgot something!" Eugene said, slapping his forehead.

"Eugene and I have to talk," Laura said, pulling Eugene's arm. "Is that the den over there?"

"Talk?" Jenny said. So Laura planned to use this opportunity to make out with Eugene.

"Yeah. That's the den. Great seeing you, Laura," she said sarcastically.

Laura just giggled.

"You guys all have to leave in a couple of hours," Jenny told them. "If Mr. Hagen comes home early and finds you here, I'll be out of here — for good!"

Chuck took Jenny's hand. "Don't worry. I'll make sure we all get out in time." He pulled her over to the couch. Laura and Eugene disappeared into the den and closed the door.

"Wonder what they're talking about," Chuck joked, looking toward the den. Then he suddenly turned serious. "Why'd you want me to bring them?"

"I didn't know about Eugene. I just thought Laura was coming. I already told you, I thought it would be more fun to study — "

"I had a feeling maybe you didn't want to be alone with me."

Jenny realized that she had underestimated how smart Chuck was, and how sensitive. "No, I — "

"I really want you to trust me, Jenny." He was still holding her hand. He squeezed it gently.

I'd really like to trust you, Chuck, she thought. I'd really like to trust you more than anything — but I don't know if I can.

He kissed her, softly at first, then harder, pulling her closer to him.

He couldn't be the one who's threatening me, she thought, kissing him back, trying to lose herself in the kiss, trying not to think about anything but him. It has to be Willers. It has to be.

But what about the note in her bag? Willers couldn't have put it there.

Chuck wrapped her in his arms and kissed her again. But she couldn't stop thinking. She couldn't stop doubting him, wondering about him, wondering. . . .

"Hey, Chuck — you left your headlights on." Eugene's head popped out from the den door.

"What?"

"I can see from the den window. Your headlights. They're on."

"Thanks, Eugene." Chuck disentangled himself from Jenny and climbed to his feet. "Sorry. I'll be right back." He headed quickly to the front door. "Save my place!"

Why did I let them come? Why did I do this? Jenny thought, watching Chuck disappear out the front door. Do I *want* to lose my job? Do I *want* Mr. Hagen to fire me so I don't have to be scared anymore?

Then she heard a sound. A footstep? A door opening?

It came from the direction of the kitchen.

Had Mr. Hagen come home early again?

Or was it a different visitor?

Company's coming.

Was this the night?

Was the kitchen door locked? She hadn't checked. Was someone in the house? She listened. Another sound.

Without realizing it, she was on her feet. Then she was in the back hallway. She walked quickly past the laundry room, past the small pantry, then slowed as she approached the kitchen.

"Who is it?" she called.

Silence.

"Hello? Anyone there?"

Chuck — please — hurry back. What's taking you so long?

The kitchen was silent, except for the loud hum of the refrigerator and the steady *plink plink plink* of water dripping from the kitchen faucet.

Was someone hiding in that silence?

Was someone waiting in that silence?

She crept a little closer, keeping near to the wall in the narrow hallway.

She tried to convince herself that she was being silly, that she was acting like a frightened child.

But she realized that her fear was justified. The phone calls had been real. The threats had been real. Willers prowling about in the garage, following her from the bus had been real.

She had real reasons to be afraid, real reasons to be cautious, to hesitate there in the hallway. This wasn't her imagination acting up again.

A sudden flash of memory. She was a little girl, seven or eight. Her parents had just divorced. She was adjusting to the sudden emptiness, the strange feeling of life with one parent where a short while before, there had been two.

She was standing in the hallway outside the kitchen door, in the old house before she and her mother moved to the house they had now. The memory was so clear, so bright, still so fresh in her mind.

A drop of blood. She spotted a bright red drop of blood on the hallway floor just outside the kitchen. Her mother was in the kitchen. She listened. She heard a chopping sound, a horrible sound, a sound she didn't recognize.

She stared at the drop of blood, glowing so red on the dark linoleum. She listened to the chop, chop, chop coming from the kitchen, so insistent, so steady, so mechanical.

She could still remember the terror from those long years ago.

What was making that chopping sound?

Why was there blood on the hallway floor?

Where was her mother? What had happened to her mother?

Propelled by her fear, she had burst into the kitchen, prepared to scream, to cry out her terror.

Her mother was standing at the sink, chopping carrots with a large knife.

Chop chop chop.

She had a Band-Aid on her thumb.

"Ma — the blood!" Jenny had screamed. She had to scream. She had to let it out. Even though her eyes told her everything was okay, she still had all that terror to let out.

"I cut my thumb," her mother said, holding the thumb up for a second for Jenny to see, then returning to the knife and the pile of carrots. Chop, chop, chop.

Clink clink clink.

Water dripped into the Hagens' kitchen sink.

The memory faded slowly. Then, propelled by the same fear she had felt as a little girl, Jenny burst into the kitchen.

No one there.

Except for the cat. The cat had knocked over the sugar cannister on the counter and was busily lapping herself into a sugar coma!

That explained the noise. Jenny ran to the kitchen door. It was locked. She leaned against the counter to catch her breath. "Got me again, kitty," she told the cat. "You bad cat." The cat ignored her and kept lapping up the sugar.

Feeling relieved, Jenny walked back to the living room. Chuck was waiting for her on the sofa. "Where'd you go?"

"Oh, I had to check on something in the kitchen," she told him.

"Come here and warm me up. It's freezing out there." He patted the sofa cushion beside him.

She was glad he was there. Her doubts about him were melting away. He genuinely liked her, he really cared about her, she thought. She had been foolish for suspecting him.

She dropped down beside him. He pulled her close.

She felt so safe now, so warm, so good.

The time seemed to fly by. She lost all track of time. She lost all track of everything.

She was still locked in Chuck's arms, still kissing him, when she looked up and saw Mr. Hagen glaring down at them from behind the sofa.

Chapter 18

He was standing so still, glaring at them with such a frozen face, his eyes unmoving, unblinking, clenched fists held straight down at his sides, that at first, Jenny thought he wasn't real. At first, she thought it was a statue, some sort of mannequin made to look like Mr. Hagen.

But as he opened his mouth to roar out his alarmed protest, she realized that he was real. And that she was caught.

Mr. Hagen lunged forward as if to grab Jenny and Chuck, his face reddening with rage. But before he could make a sound, before he got more than a step or two, Mrs. Hagen walked into the room. Her mouth dropped open in surprise. "Jenny? Who — ?"

Mr. Hagen stopped short. He was breathing heavily.

"Hey — what's going on?" Eugene called. He and Laura walked out quickly from the den.

"Uh-oh," Laura said, realizing at once what

147

was happening. Her lipstick was smeared all over her chin.

Mrs. Hagen ran immediately to her husband and put a hand on his shoulder, more to comfort him than restrain him. "It's okay, dear. It's okay," she said softly. "Jenny's friends will go home now. Then we'll have a quiet talk with Jenny about this."

She didn't remove her hand until Mr. Hagen seemed to calm down a little. He took a step back. He was still glaring at Jenny. He hadn't said a word.

"I'm sorry. I'm really sorry," Jenny said, jumping to her feet. "My friends stopped by to keep me company and — "

"We were just going," Chuck said, motioning to Laura and Eugene. He looked really frightened of Mr. Hagen. They all did. Mr. Hagen looked truly scary, as if it was taking all of his power to keep himself under control.

"I could drive Jenny home," Chuck said to Mrs. Hagen.

"Yes — " Jenny agreed quickly. "Save you a trip," she told Mr. Hagen. He didn't seem to hear her.

"No. You three go on ahead," Mrs. Hagen said, still holding on to her husband's broad shoulder. "I think we'll want to have a little talk with Jenny first."

"I'm really sorry," Chuck whispered to Jenny. "I'll wait for you at your house. Okay?"

She nodded, keeping her eyes on Mr. Hagen,

who seemed to be getting over his shock and rage.

"Let's go up and check on Donny," Mrs. Hagen suggested brightly to her husband. "Nothing terrible has happened here."

He nodded. "I guess you're right." The first words he had said. He let his wife lead him to the stairs.

She knows how to calm him down, Jenny thought. She's probably had to do this before. It's going to be okay. I'm going to be fired, but that's okay, too. I didn't really want this baby-sitting job anymore.

Her three friends, giving her looks of regret, hurried out the door. Jenny stood alone in the living room for a while, telling herself that nothing terrible had happened, that it was mostly embarrassing, that's all. No crime had been committed.

She decided to get her coat from the upstairs closet so that she'd be ready for Mr. Hagen to take her home. She climbed the stairs and entered the Hagens' large bedroom. It was lit by a single lamp on a table beside their four-poster bed. The closet was against the far wall on the other side of the bed.

I'm in for a long lecture from Mr. Hagen, Jenny told herself. But then at least I'll be out of here for good. She realized she'd miss Donny. But she wouldn't miss anything else. Wow, did Mr. Hagen look mad! He was going to have to do something to control his temper!

She slid open the closet door and searched for her down jacket among all the clothes. The closet smelled of Mrs. Hagen's perfume, strong and flowery. The hangers were all full. Jenny spotted her jacket on a high shelf above the hangers.

Reaching up on tiptoe to pull it down, she knocked a cardboard shoe box off the shelf. The box hit the closet floor and bounced open, the lid flying onto Jenny's sneakers.

Bending down to put the box back together, she was surprised to see that it was stuffed with newspaper clippings. She started to replace the lid, but then some headlines caught her eye:

BABY-SITTER ATTACK REPORTED ON EAST SIDE.

BABY-SITTER BLAMED IN BABY'S DROWNING.

Jenny felt a cold chill run down her back. Her hands shaking, her heart beginning to pound, she riffled through the clippings.

POLICE ISSUE WARNINGS AFTER THIRD BABY-SITTER ATTACK.

BABY-SITTER ADMITS TO KIDNAP-PING CHILD.

BABY-SITTER RESPONSIBLE FOR CHILD'S DEATH.

All of the neatly clipped articles were about baby-sitters, Jenny realized. Dozens and dozens of clippings. All about baby-sitters and the recent attacks on baby-sitters.

It was too dark by the closet to read the clippings, and her hands were shaking too badly, but Jenny noticed that certain words had been circled in red. She picked up the box and pulled out a few clippings to see more clearly.

The names.

The baby-sitters' names had been circled in red marker.

"No!" Jenny gasped.

She dropped the box to the floor, the clippings scattering across the rug.

Mr. Hagen — why has he collected these? He must be CRAZY! she told herself. I've got to get out of here!

She picked up her jacket and started to turn away from the closet. "Oh!" She cried aloud when she realized Mr. Hagen was standing right behind her.

Did he see the box of clippings? Did he see that she had discovered the box?

"Ready to go home?" he asked, pulling on his black leather gloves.

She couldn't tell. He looked very calm now. She stood up quickly and closed the closet door. Maybe he hadn't noticed that the box was down on the floor. It was pretty dark down there, after all.

"Ready?" he repeated.

"No. Uh . . . It's so far for you to drive, Mr. Hagen, and you look so tired," she said, thinking frantically. "Why don't I take the bus tonight?"

He shook his head no.

She didn't want to ride with him. Not now. Not ever again. Not after seeing his collection of baby-sitter stories.

The question repeated in her mind as she

stared back at him in the dim light: Did he know she had seen the clippings? Had he seen the open box on the closet floor?

She couldn't tell.

"I won't hear of it, Jenny," he said, taking her coat out of her hands and helping her into it. His steel-gray eyes burned into hers, revealing nothing. "I won't hear of it. You're coming with me."

"Really, Mr. Hagen. I don't mind — "

He frowned, turned, and headed to the stairs. "Let's go," he said quietly.

Chapter 19

"Good night, Jenny. See you Thursday," Mrs. Hagen called from Donny's room. "Mike — don't lecture her all the way home!"

Jenny wanted to stop and call to her for help. "Please don't make me ride with him!" she wanted to say. "I think he's crazy. I saw the clippings! Please — don't make me ride home with him!"

But she stopped herself. "Good night, Mrs. Hagen," she called softly.

She scolded herself for letting her imagination run away with her. What did the clippings mean anyway? Sure, Mr. Hagen was nervous and excitable. But he had always seemed very sweet underneath his nervousness. And he certainly did love his child.

There were a lot of reasons why he might have kept those clippings, she told herself. It didn't necessarily mean he was a sicko.

She was feeling a little better by the time she climbed into the front seat of the car. Mr. Hagen smiled at her as he closed her door.

I'm just completely exhausted, she thought. I've got to calm down now. It's all over. All of the creepiness is over.

"Quite a night, huh?" Mr. Hagen said, shaking his head as he climbed behind the wheel. "Quite a night."

He backed down the drive and headed up Edgetown Lane. Jenny rested her head against the seatback and wearily closed her eyes. A loud click made her open them. Mr. Hagen had touched a control button and locked all the doors.

Funny, Jenny thought. He's never done that before.

She settled back again, determined not to imagine any new terrors. There was nothing wrong with locking the car doors, after all. In fact, it was considerate of him.

She closed her eyes again. He was silent, not questioning her about her friends, not lecturing her. What was he waiting for?

When she opened her eyes a few moments later, she didn't recognize where they were. "Is this Millertown Road?" she asked, peering out into the darkness.

"No," he answered softly.

She waited for him to tell her what road it was, but he drove on in silence. Outside the frosty window, there were no houses or stores. She made out an occasional barn and silo, and farm houses as dark and silent as the fields that surrounded them.

"Where are we? We seem to be heading out

of town!" she said, sitting straight up, no longer tired.

He didn't say anything. He kept his eyes straight ahead on the flat, uncurving road.

"Mr. Hagen — why are we going this way?" Her voice revealed her growing fear.

"I'm going very fast," he said finally. "I wouldn't try anything if I were you."

"What?" She wasn't sure she heard him correctly. He couldn't have said that — could he??

She leaned forward to look at the speedometer. He was doing 85.

"Mr. Hagen — please — "

"I'm sorry you saw my clippings," he said, his eyes straight ahead, his voice even, emotionless, almost machinelike. "But it really doesn't matter."

"I — I didn't see anything," she lied. It didn't sound at all convincing. "Please — where are you taking me?"

I've got to get out of here, she thought. But how?

"Please, Mr. Hagen," she said, forcing her voice down, forcing herself not to cry, not to scream. "Please take me home now."

He drove on in silence, his large hands at the top of the wheel.

He's crazy, she thought.

He's crazy and he's out of control.

Where is he taking me? What does he plan to do?

I'm going to get away. I'm going to be okay.

She repeated those words again and again,

staring out the window at the shifting night shadows. They were way out of town now, and heading farther out, roaring toward the empty flatlands where the fields ended, where no trees grew, where no one lived, where no one went unless they were on their way somewhere else.

"Company's coming," Mr. Hagen whispered, staring straight ahead, talking to himself, smiling a strangely satisfied smile. "Don't worry. Company's coming."

"It was YOU!" Jenny screamed.

"SHUT UP!" he yelled with sudden fury. He raised his left hand from the wheel and slapped her face, a stinging blow.

The loud sound of it surprised her more than the slap itself. Pain shot up her head and down her neck. She was too hurt, too shocked, too frightened to scream.

"I tried to warn you," he whispered, the hoarse whisper she had heard on the phone. "But now you'll get what's coming to you."

"But I didn't *do* anything!" Jenny cried. Her head throbbed like a giant toothache. She turned away and stared out the side window, as if not seeing him might make him disappear, might make this entire nightmare disappear.

"I had a baby," Mr. Hagen said, still in that hoarse whisper, talking to himself now. "I had a baby. A little girl. She was only two. But the baby-sitter wasn't quick enough. The baby-sitter wasn't smart enough. The baby-sitter wasn't GOOD ENOUGH!"

Jenny didn't turn around, didn't reply, didn't

react in any way. She remembered the girl in the photograph, the girl who looked just like Donny.

"My little girl died," Mr. Hagen said. "Now it's your turn."

Her head hit the dashboard as he slammed on the brakes.

The car squealed for several hundred yards, sliding over smooth ground, then finally stopped.

When Jenny looked up, he was already pulling open the door, already grabbing her, jerking her out of the car.

"Let go," she said, just mouthing the words, an almost silent plea. He was too strong. There was no way she could fight him.

He slapped her again, this time catching her jaw, snapping her head back.

Then he grabbed her by the shoulders and shoved her in front of the car, into the bright cylinders of light from the headlights. "Move!" he ordered, pushing her shoulders.

She stumbled and started to fall, but he pulled her up. Her eyes adjusted slowly to the bright light. She was walking on solid rock now.

Two more steps, three more. She realized where he had taken her. It was the quarry. The old rock quarry, about ten miles out of town. The quarry had been deserted for years.

There wasn't a sound. There didn't seem to be air to breathe.

The world was silent, except for their shoes moving over the hard rock surface as he pushed her toward the quarry.

The headlights shot out in two straight beams. Then the light suddenly vanished.

"No!" Jenny cried aloud.

She realized why the light suddenly stopped. It stopped at the edge of the quarry, the edge of the deep, empty pit.

"Move!" Mr. Hagen repeated, giving her a hard shove that took her right to the edge, to where the light stopped.

She looked down. It was a sheer drop, hundreds of feet down to jagged rocks below.

"This is what you deserve, Jenny," he screamed.

"I didn't kill any baby!" Jenny cried.

The look on Mr. Hagen's face was almost as terrifying as the thought of the quarry. It went beyond cold. It went beyond hatred. It went beyond inhuman.

He looked like one of those hideous undead monsters that stagger through the horror movies, eyes ablaze with fury, everything else about them zombielike and dead.

"I had a baby. This is what you deserve."

He didn't move his lips when he talked. He didn't blink.

"I didn't do anything!" Jenny's voice came out in a desperate cry.

"It's time to die."

"No! Mr. Hagen — please!"

She knew he couldn't hear her. His face was no longer alive. Even his eyes had narrowed and nearly closed. It was as if he were retreating, pulling into himself, so that he wouldn't see what he was about to do to her.

"No — please!"

"Good-bye, Jenny."

"No! Think about Donny! Think about — "

"Do you want to jump now. Or should I push you?"

What? Was he giving her a choice? Was this her opportunity to stall?

"Choose fast, Jenny. Jump or be pushed?"

"Mr. Hagen, listen to me — "

"Okay. That's your choice. You choose to be pushed."

He raised his arms and moved forward, his eyes still dead, his face expressionless.

Jenny backed up. She was on the very edge now. Her left heel rested on air. She nearly toppled backwards, down, down into the deep pit, onto the rocks so far below.

Struggling to regain her balance, to get back on firm footing, she tried to inch forward, but he wouldn't let her. He came toward her slowly, preparing to push her back. A smile spread across his face. He was enjoying her fear.

"Stop right there, Hagen!"

A man's voice from behind the car.

Mr. Hagen spun around, startled. Jenny stared into the headlights. She couldn't see. The lights were blinding. She looked away, bright yellow circles following wherever she looked.

"Who's there?" Mr. Hagen called, peering into the darkness.

A man stepped in front of the headlights.

Jenny blinked, trying to clear her eyes, trying to see who it was.

She saw the plaid wool lumberjack shirt.

Willers!

What did he want? Did he want to kill her, too?

Willers raised the pistol in his hand. He moved a few steps closer.

"What are you doing here?" Mr. Hagen shouted angrily.

"Saving you from ruining your life," Willers shouted back, brandishing the pistol.

Mr. Hagen threw back his head and laughed, a crazy, exaggerated laugh.

Jenny tried to move away from the edge of the quarry. But he was still blocking her way. She felt dizzy. Her head was spinning. She didn't know how much longer she could stand with nothing but air behind her.

"My life is already ruined," Mr. Hagen said bitterly.

"I can't do anything about that, Hagen," Willers said, taking another cautious step forward. "But I can stop you from committing a murder."

"No, you can't," Mr. Hagen told him.

He lunged toward Jenny and gave her a hard push.

Chapter 20

Jenny dodged to the left and collapsed to the ground.

Mr. Hagen sailed over her and plunged over the quarry side.

His scream cut through the air like a fading police siren. Then she heard a sickening crash, like a full carton of eggs hitting the sidewalk.

Then silence.

It happened so quickly it didn't seem real to her.

She looked up, expecting him to still be there, standing over her, his small, gray eyes burning into hers with such insane hatred.

But she saw only headlights.

Then two legs in front of the headlights, legs walking quickly toward her.

Then Willers's dark stubbled face was down low near hers.

"Are you okay? Can you get up?"

The words didn't make any sense at first. The siren was still blaring in her ears. The short siren of Mr. Hagen's scream followed by the cracking sound, the sound of his body hitting the rocks below. What language was this man speaking? What was she doing out here on the edge of the old quarry in the middle of the night?

And then suddenly, as Willers stared down at her, as he offered his hand to help her up, the words made sense. "Yes. I'm okay," she said, a little surprised that she could form words herself.

What did she expect?

Did she expect to be dead right now?

Yes. That was it. She expected to be dead.

But someone else was.

Mr. Hagen was dead. Down at the bottom of the quarry.

She climbed to her feet. "I'm not hurt," she told Willers.

Even in this strange, harsh light from the car headlights, he looked very shaken. "I — I tried to stop him," he said, his voice trembling. He took Jenny's arm. She thought he was trying to help support her, but she quickly realized he wanted to lean on her.

"I tried to stop him. I tried to save him."

"There was nothing you could do," Jenny said softly, ignoring the smell of stale cigar smoke that clung to Willers's shirt.

Jenny shivered. The air was cold and wet, and she was perspiring from the horror of her close call. Holding onto her arm, Willers began to lead her to his car, which was parked in the darkness behind Mr. Hagen's car. Along the way, he stopped and turned off Mr. Hagen's headlights, plunging them into total darkness. Jenny looked up to the sky. There was no moon.

She made her way slowly, her eyes adjusting to the dark. She listened to the crunch of her sneakers over the hard ground. She had never realized how good that sound could be, so solid, so real, so alive.

"I should introduce myself," Willers said, stopping in front of his battered old Honda Civic. "You probably guessed that my name isn't Willers and I'm not the next-door neighbor."

"Yeah," Jenny said, shivering. She reached for the door handle. She wanted to get inside the car where it was warmer.

"My name is Ferris. Lieutenant Ferris."

"You're the policeman?"

"That's right. I'm with the town police. I was assigned to this case."

"C-can we g-get into the car?" Jenny stammered. "I'm not feeling too well."

"Oh. Sorry." He pulled open the door for her and she collapsed into the tiny bucket seat. The car started reluctantly. Ferris let it warm up for a while, then pulled out onto the road.

"Where are you taking me? The police station?" Jenny asked, shaking all over, unable to get warm.

"No. I'm going to take you home," Ferris said. "I think you've had enough excitement for one night."

"How did you know to — how did you know he — ?"

"I've had Hagen's house staked out for a

month. When the complaints started — "

"Complaints?"

"Well, I should say attacks. The attacks on baby-sitters. I was assigned the case."

"Baby-sitters. Mr. Hagen had clippings about them all," Jenny said. Her head was spinning with images, frightening images, pictures of everything that had happened that night.

Ferris looked at her, surprised. "Clippings?"

"Up in his closet."

Ferris shook his head. "He was one of the main suspects right from the beginning. Two years ago, his daughter died mysteriously. No one ever knew the cause. He went berserk. He blamed the baby-sitter who was taking care of her. It wasn't the girl's fault, but Hagen just went nuts. He attacked the girl, beat her up pretty badly. It went to court. He got off lightly because he had been in a disturbed emotional state.

"Then he moved to the other side of town and took a new job. When someone started beating up baby-sitters a few months ago, he was our prime suspect."

"When you chased after me at the bus stop — " Jenny started, trying to get it clear, trying to clear her mind from the whirling, confused images.

"I tried to warn you," Ferris said, eyes on the road. "But then when you ran, I changed my mind. I wanted to see what Hagen had planned."

"You used me?"

He was silent for a while. "Yeah. I guess you could say that."

"But how could you do that to me?" she cried, suddenly angry.

"Give me a break," he muttered, a low growl. Her question seemed to hurt him. "This didn't turn out the way I'd hoped. Believe me."

Jenny realized she shouldn't be angry at Ferris. He was just doing his job. Besides, he had saved her life.

Her life.

She was alive.

And Mr. Hagen was lying crushed and crumpled at the bottom of the quarry.

"His poor family," she said, her voice a choked whisper.

"Poor everybody," Ferris said bitterly.

He stopped the car, shifted into park, and pulled on the handbrake.

"Why are you stopping?" Jenny asked suspiciously.

He gave her a weary smile. "You're home."

She looked out. They were in her driveway.

Ferris walked her to the door, then followed her inside as Jenny's mother greeted her with a long, emotional hug. "You're okay? Where were you? Chuck said he left the Hagens' over an hour ago."

"I've been worried out of my head," Chuck said, appearing suddenly from the kitchen and putting his arm around Jenny.

"This is Lieutenant Ferris," Jenny said. "It's all a long story, a long, frightening story. But it's over. Could I have some tea? I can't stop shaking."

As Mrs. Jeffers hurried to make tea, Ferris told them quickly what had happened. After asking Jenny at least a dozen times if she really was okay, her relieved mother hugged her again and, looking dazed, dropped down onto a kitchen chair. "Such a sad story," she muttered, shaking her head.

"It's a very sad story," Ferris said softly. "And it's going to get sadder. Now I have to go tell Mrs. Hagen what happened." He shook his head, then turned to Jenny. "I'll pick you up tomorrow and bring you to the police station to make a statement, okay? In the meantime, get some rest."

After Ferris left, the three of them settled down in the warm kitchen, sitting at the bright yellow Formica counter, drinking soothing hot tea with honey. Conversation was awkward. They were each thinking of what a close call Jenny had had that night.

"It's good to be here," Jenny said finally, sipping the fragrant tea.

"Yeah," Chuck agreed. "This is a nice kitchen."

"I meant it's good to be alive," Jenny said, smiling at him.

"Oh. Right," Chuck said, embarrassed.

"I have the feeling things are going to be good from now on," Jenny said, still looking at Chuck. "I don't think I'll live in such a fantasy world anymore, letting my imagination run away with me all the time. The real world is interesting enough!"

"A reality trip," Chuck said, smiling back at her.

"I guess there's something to be learned, even in such a terrible tragedy," Mrs. Jeffers said. "But the important thing is that you're safe. You're here. You're all right. Oh. I almost forgot." She put her mug down hard on the counter. "Mrs. Milton — you know, down the block with the twins? She called tonight, Jenny. She wants to know if you can baby-sit next week."

Jenny stared at her mother in disbelief. "Mother, I — well, I — No. I don't think so. I think maybe I'll give it a miss."

"That's right," Chuck said, taking Jenny's hand. "She has a steady baby-sitting job on Friday nights, Mrs. Jeffers."

"What?" Jenny's mother looked very confused.

"From now on, she's baby-sitting me!" Chuck said.

Chuck was the only one who laughed.

"Thank you, Chuck," Jenny said. "That was the perfect dreadful joke to end a perfectly dreadful evening." She pulled him up from the counter and, holding his hands tightly and leaning wearily against him, she walked him to the door to say good night.

About the Author

R.L. STINE is the author of more than 60 books of humor and adventure for young people, and was formerly an editor of humor magazines at Scholastic. He lives and works in New York City with his wife, Jane, and his son, Matthew. Lately most of his energy has gone into writing scary novels for teenager readers. *The Baby-sitter* is his seventh young adult novel.

THRILLERS

Nobody Scares 'Em Like R.L. Stine

THRILLERS

D.E. Athkins
☐ MC45246-0 Mirror, Mirror $3.25
☐ MC45349-1 The Ripper $3.25

A. Bates
☐ MC45829-9 The Dead Game $3.25
☐ MC43291-5 Final Exam $3.25
☐ MC44582-0 Mother's Helper $3.25
☐ MC44238-4 Party Line $3.25

Caroline B. Cooney
☐ MC44316-X The Cheerleader $3.25
☐ MC41641-3 The Fire $3.25
☐ MC43806-9 The Fog $3.25
☐ MC45681-4 Freeze Tag $3.25
☐ MC45402-1 The Perfume $3.25
☐ MC44884-6 The Return of the
Vampire $2.95
☐ MC41640-5 The Snow $3.99
☐ MC45680-6 The Stranger $3.50
☐ MC45682-2 The Vampire's
Promise $3.50

Richie Tankersley Cusick
☐ MC43115-3 April Fools $3.25
☐ MC43203-6 The Lifeguard $3.25
☐ MC43114-5 Teacher's Pet $3.25
☐ MC44235-X Trick or Treat $3.50

Carol Ellis
☐ MC46411-6 Camp Fear $3.25
☐ MC44768-8 My Secret Admirer $3.25
☐ MC47101-5 Silent Witness $3.25
☐ MC46044-7 The Stepdaughter $3.25
☐ MC44916-8 The Window $3.25

Lael Littke
☐ MC44237-6 Prom Dress $3.50

Jane McFann
☐ MC46090-9 Be Mine $3.25

Christopher Pike
☐ MC43014-9 Slumber Party $3.50
☐ MC44256-2 Weekend $3.50

Edited by T. Pines
☐ MC45256-8 Thirteen $3.99

Sinclair Smith
☐ MC45063-8 The Waitress $3.50

Barbara Steiner
☐ MC46425-6 The Phantom $3.50

Robert Westall
☐ MC41693-6 Ghost Abbey $3.25
☐ MC43761-5 The Promise $3.25
☐ MC45176-6 Yaxley's Cat $3.25

Available wherever you buy books, or use this order form.

Scholastic Inc., P.O. Box 7502, 2931 East McCarty Street, Jefferson City, MO 65102

Please send me the books I have checked above. I am enclosing $_____ (please add $2.00 to cover shipping and handling). Send check or money order — no cash or C.O.D.s please.

Name _____ Age _____

Address_____

City_____ State/Zip_____

Please allow four to six weeks for delivery. Offer good in the U.S. only. Sorry, mail orders are not available to residents of Canada. Prices subject to change. T295

WARNING Thrillers by **Diane Hoh** contain irresistible ingredients which may be hazardous to your peace of mind!

☐ BAP44330-5	**The Accident**		$3.25
☐ BAP45401-3	**The Fever**		$3.25
☐ BAP43050-5	**Funhouse**		$3.25
☐ BAP44904-4	**The Invitation**		$3.25
☐ BAP45640-7	**The Train**		$3.25

Available wherever you buy books, or use this order form.